ABSOLUTE FORCE

(A JAKE MERCER POLITICAL THRILLER—BOOK 3)

JACK MARS

Jack Mars

Jack Mars is the USA Today bestselling author of the LUKE STONE thriller series, which includes seven books. He is also the author of the new FORGING OF LUKE STONE prequel series, comprising six books; of the AGENT ZERO spy thriller series, comprising twelve books; of the TROY STARK thriller series, comprising seven books; of the SPY GAME thriller series, comprising nine books; and of the new JAKE MERCER thriller series, comprising five books (and counting).

Jack loves to hear from you, so please feel free to visit www.Jackmarsauthor.com to join the email list, receive a free book, receive free giveaways, connect on Facebook and Twitter, and stay in touch!

ISBN: 978-1-0943-8553-2

BOOKS BY JACK MARS

JAKE MERCER THRILLER SERIES
ABSOLUTE THREAT (Book #1)
ABSOLUTE DAMAGE (Book #2)
ABSOLUTE FORCE (Book #3)
ABSOLUTE PERIL (Book #4)
ABSOLUTE TREASON (Book #5)

THE SPY GAME
TARGET ONE (Book #1)
TARGET TWO (Book #2)
TARGET THREE (Book #3)
TARGET FOUR (Book #4)
TARGET FIVE (Book #5)
TARGET SIX (Book #6)
TARGET SEVEN (Book #7)
TARGET EIGHT (Book #8)

TROY STARK THRILLER SERIES
ROGUE FORCE (Book #1)
ROGUE COMMAND (Book #2)
ROGUE TARGET (Book #3)
ROGUE MISSION (Book #4)
ROGUE SHOT (Book #5)
ROGUE STRIKE (Book #6)
ROGUE ORDER (Book #7)

LUKE STONE THRILLER SERIES
ANY MEANS NECESSARY (Book #1)
OATH OF OFFICE (Book #2)
SITUATION ROOM (Book #3)
OPPOSE ANY FOE (Book #4)
PRESIDENT ELECT (Book #5)
OUR SACRED HONOR (Book #6)
HOUSE DIVIDED (Book #7)

FORGING OF LUKE STONE PREQUEL SERIES

PRIMARY TARGET (Book #1)
PRIMARY COMMAND (Book #2)
PRIMARY THREAT (Book #3)
PRIMARY GLORY (Book #4)
PRIMARY VALOR (Book #5)
PRIMARY DUTY (Book #6)

AN AGENT ZERO SPY THRILLER SERIES

AGENT ZERO (Book #1)
TARGET ZERO (Book #2)
HUNTING ZERO (Book #3)
TRAPPING ZERO (Book #4)
FILE ZERO (Book #5)
RECALL ZERO (Book #6)
ASSASSIN ZERO (Book #7)
DECOY ZERO (Book #8)
CHASING ZERO (Book #9)
VENGEANCE ZERO (Book #10)
ZERO ZERO (Book #11)
ABSOLUTE ZERO (Book #12)

PROLOGUE

"The fact that we're even having a conversation about near-peer adversaries is a problem," General Hawks said. "There shouldn't be such a thing. Our supremacy should be utterly unchallenged. So why the hell are we squabbling over budgets?"

The others gathered around wisely said nothing.

All meetings were treated as though they were critical, but in Harold Grant's experience, most weren't. He'd been to too many meetings. He'd been to enough meetings to make him wonder if he ought to rethink his career entirely. Senator Nat Barello seemed to make every meeting a priority, and of course, Harold was the aide stuck joining him. Every. Damned. Time.

His role at this meeting, as at every other meeting, was to pretend not to hear anything being said while also making sure to commit everything to memory. That way, if Senator Barello needed a piece of information later on, Harold would be able to provide it to him.

This meeting, however, actually appeared critical. Normally, an aide wouldn't be allowed in a meeting like this, but Senator Barello served on the Senate Armed Services committee, and at Barello's request, Harold had been extensively vetted and given clearance. That didn't mean he knew everything, though. Harold had been to many secure locations with the senator in the past, but this was easily the most secure place of all of them. Harold didn't even know where it was.

He knew he was in an underground bunker in a large conference room with screens all over the walls. He had caught glimpses of other parts of the facility and had seen enough to piece together that this was some sort of weapons research lab, but he had chosen not to follow that thought through to any conclusions. Even for a walking prop like an aide, knowing too much could be dangerous.

And clearly, the government didn't want people to know much about this place. The level of security was impressive. He'd had his fingerprint and retina scanned before he was even allowed onto the aboveground outpost that led to this bunker. He'd been through two metal detectors, one x-ray machine, and stood for almost five minutes while three different agents checked him for recording devices in a manner that would have justified a legal complaint in any other circumstance.

But eventually, he had made it to the conference room, and now he stood and tried to appear to notice nothing. He noticed everything, though. Perhaps the strangest thing to notice was that his boss was nobody important here. Oh, his boss was a very important man, but the others in this room were far more important. The ranking member of the Senate Intelligence Committee was here. A deputy director of the CIA was here. Officially, he was several steps removed, but in reality, he was the de facto director of the CIA and had been for the last fifteen years.

The Secretary of Homeland Security wasn't here, which is unsurprising given his recent political challenges. Six months ago, a terrorist organization had executed three different assassination attempts in Washington D.C. within the span of two weeks. None of the attempts had been successful, but they had resulted in the deaths of over two dozen federal agents and nearly one hundred civilians, so needless to say, the Secretary was waist-deep in a knee-deep pool of shit. The Deputy Secretary was here, though, along with the Speaker of the House.

The real power here, though, the man in charge, the man running the meeting, held more real power—at least when it came to national defense policy—than anyone but the President. General Antony L. Hawks, the United States Secretary of Defense, sat at the head of the table. Everyone deferred to him, even those who criticized him politically.

Harold was a little surprised to see him. General Hawks was notorious for avoiding meetings. Unless your title was Mr. President, he was all but impossible to see.

Harold saw him now, though. He was unsurprised to discover that Hawks' reputation for irascibility and impatience was well-earned. The few attendees who risked trying to bullshit him very quickly learned how little he tolerated such nonsense. Harold was glad he was essentially a nonperson here. He would have hated to be on the receiving end of one of Hawks' tirades.

The meeting topic was international arms reduction, a favorite topic among politicians because it got press, but somehow no one ever expected a solution. It had been used to win elections for sixty years. Like taxes, welfare reform, and health insurance, it was one of many political issues neither Congress nor the Executive Branch had any real desire to solve.

For General Hawks to be here, though, something real was in the works. That made this meeting not only critical but interesting.

Before the truly interesting part of the meeting began, though, the ground shook. The meeting came to a halt as everyone struggled to determine if they had felt what they thought they felt.

They did. Then they felt it again. Harold blinked, and when he opened his eyes, he wasn't looking at the head of the table anymore, but at the ceiling. A tile was missing. He fixated on the hole in the ceiling where that tile had been and tried to work out why that was important.

Then faces replaced the tile, a great many faces, all staring at him. That wasn't good. He was supposed to be invisible. Why were people noticing him?

And Why couldn't he hear anything even though their mouths were moving? Nat Barello got up and rushed to him. There was concern in his eyes. Worry. Nat Barello had never been worried or concerned about anyone.

"Hal!" the senator shouted. "Hal, hang on Buddy! Just hang on!"

He turned his head in wonder and saw himself on the screen. His face didn't really matter much to him, but the metal pole through his body seemed important. He stared at it and tried to understand how he could see it there. Then, he looked down and saw it in front of him. It didn't belong there! It didn't belong there!

He reached down to take hold of it. The moment his hands closed over the metal, his senses returned to him. He didn't want them. He screamed as pain rushed over him. He could still hear himself screaming as darkness took him.

***

"What the hell are you doing?" the man screamed. He was a nobody. Leo wasn't even certain the man could be called an aide instead of a page.

"Get back to your congressman and wait there," Leo said.

"While you do nothing? What the hell are you doing?"

Leo forced himself to take a deep breath before saying, "There are a dozen people here we have to protect, and I'm sorry to say that you're very low on the priority list. So if you want any chance of getting out of here alive, you'll do what I say when I say it. So, get your ass back to your congressman and wait for instructions. Is that clear?"

The man nodded, but before he could move, a second shockwave followed the first, and he fell to the floor. Leo angrily lifted him to his feet and shoved him toward the open door. "Go! Go!" he said.

He heard gunfire behind him and turned around. A quick rush out of the other door brought him to the firefight. There were six other Secret Service agents, and a man in battle dress uniform, General Hawks' aide. He looked at Leo and said, "The man at the computer is Hadad."

The man at the computer wore a suit that probably cost more than Leo's car. Not that he would know. It wasn't like he shopped for clothes at the Armani tailor.

"Hadad? Is that a terrorist organization?"

"No. It's his name. He's an arms dealer."

"Hadad what?"

"Just Hadad."

One of Hadad's men turned toward them, weapons drawn. Leo fired two rounds into the man's chest. but the man only staggered backwards. Damn it, they had body armor.

"Where are the others?" he asked.

"They're getting everyone to safety."

Hadad said, "I've got it," and backed away from the laptop. He had dark olive skin and appeared very Middle Eastern, but spoke English with a soft British accent. "Let's go."

"We can't let him leave with whatever he got," Hawks' aide said.

As a Secret Service agent, Leo's priority was to get the VIPs to safety, so leaving was absolutely his number one priority.

But Leo had fought with the Secret Service when terrorists invaded the White House, and he wasn't about to let another terrorist escape. He lifted his gun and aimed for Hadad's head.

And that was when Hadad raised his own gun. It looked more like a radar gun than an actual gun. Leo frowned at the odd weapon for a moment. Then, without warning, his insides exploded. He fell to his knees and vomited powerfully. When he lifted his head, he could see all of the others vomiting, the Secret Service agents as well as Hawks' aide.

He didn't know where his gun was. As the room glowed with red from the alarm lights and spun not only from the nausea but also from the unending, shrieking siren, Leo felt all hope disappear. He heard that same slightly accented voice say, "See. I told you this thing was powerful. They're totally screwed for another two or three minutes. Full recovery is still an hour or two away. Let's go."

Leo used every bit of willpower left inside of him to lift his gun, but he could only manage to turn his head slightly. If he couldn't stop them from getting to Hawks and the others, at least he could take one of them out.

But Hadad and his men weren't trying to get to the VIPs. Instead, they left the way they came. That didn't make any sense at all.

Leo tried to stand but fell back to his knees. He slipped and landed in a pool of his own vomit. The room strobed around him, and after a few seconds, Leo's eyes closed and he stopped trying to make sense of anything.

CHAPTER ONE

Jake Mercer imagined the best place to run was probably a mountain trail. He imagined the sound of the breeze over pine needles or the chirping of birds or squirrels would really appeal to him. There was peace and beauty in nature that he could rarely find in the city. Jogging through the National Mall wasn't exactly the same as an isolated run through nature, but it had its moments.

At the moment, he was nearing the Lincoln Memorial. He picked up speed as he got close. The once proud symbol of American unity had been freshly reconstructed and painted following the terrorist attack six months ago, but all Jake could see was the blood, and all he could hear was the screams of the dying.

He loved the Mall. History seemed truly alive here. Generations of stories were immortalized, the history and philosophy of the greatest nation in history preserved for future generations. He hated thinking of anything at the mall as ominous. He hated it with a passion.

As he got closer, he felt a stitch in his side. He cursed and tried to run through it, but the stitch quickly became a sharp pain, and he was forced to stop.

That was another thing he hated. His entire life, he'd been in good shape. After joining the Marine Corps out of high school, he'd been in phenomenal shape and remained that way.

Three months ago, however, he had nearly been killed while trying to stop a madman from unleashing biological terror on the world in the form of a supervirus. Jake had contracted the virus and been beaten and stabbed in the process of trying to stop the mad scientist responsible. While convalescing, he had fought to defend the President and his family against another terrorist raid. When he returned to the United States, he was near death. Doctors feared he would never be the same again.

His recovery had progressed by leaps and bounds so far, but standing in front of the location where it had all started with his hand clutched to his side and his breath coming in ragged, painful gasps, he was reminded painfully of how far he still had to go.

The memorial. stood silent and majestic. At least it should have. It was silent, of course, but once more, the stone memorial evoked a sense of doom rather than majesty.

God, he hated this.

"Hello, Slacker," came a familiar voice. He turned and saw his partner, Special Agent Jess Foster, approaching. Unlike Jake, she wore only jogging shorts and a sports bra despite the chilly autumn weather. The contrast between her outfit and Jake's multiple layers of warm clothing only heightened the sense of inadequacy he felt.

Jess smiled and came to a stop next to him. "Way to run, old man."

Her words stung, but he hid that reaction and only chuckled and said, "Just catching my breath."

She nodded. "I knew I'd find you here. You always run here."

For now, that was true, but after today, Jake decided that finding a mountain trail had to be a priority. "Well, you found me," he said, "What's up?"

She held out a folder to him. "This is up," she said.

He glanced at it. It was the itinerary for the President's diplomatic trip to the Middle East. He nodded and put the folder in his windbreaker.

"You don't want to go over it?" Jess asked.

"I do," he said, "so you'll have to jog with me."

"Sure you're up to that, old man?"

No. "The day I can't run is the day I shoot myself."

"Hey!" She shoved him, not entirely playfully. "Don't joke like that!"

He smiled. "All right, what are the potential threats? What do I need to know? What do I need to tell the other agents so they're more effective?" He started jogging again as soon as he got the words out.

She fell into step next to him. "That's for you to decide. You're the big strong badass Secret Service agent. I'm the hacker who performs miracles in front of a computer screen. I don't make tactical plans."

"So, what are the threats?"

"Well, we're starting in Syria for one thing, so we can reasonably expect threats from ISIS. They don't have a lot of power in the region anymore, and Russia's been doing a surprisingly good job of keeping them out of power but considering the recent challenges to our diplomatic relationship with Moscow, it's not outside of the realm of possibility that they 'accidentally' let an ISIS bomb through."

“So first things first,” Jake said, forcing himself to breathe through the pain in his side. “We have the military ensure that there’s a secure perimeter around… what city are we stopping in?”

“Damascus. You would know that if you stopped to read the itinerary.”

He rolled his eyes. “Okay, so we need the military to establish a secure perimeter around the city.”

“That might be difficult considering the tensions between the Syrian government and the U.S. government.”

“I don’t give a shit. After what happened in France, I’m not letting any other nation have a say in the President’s security.”

“All right,” Jess said, lifting a hand placatingly. “I’ll make a phone call.”

“Okay, so the city’s safe. What’s the next threat?”

“Someone inside the city, either a Syrian militant or a foreign insurgent, decides to wear a bomb vest or use a sniper rifle. Or any kind of weapon, really.”

Jake suspected that was a far more serious risk than anything else they might run into. “Okay, so the answer to that is the President is surrounded at all times by agents and no one—and I mean no one, gets closer to him than the outside of a very thick wall of other bodies. If we see so much as a whiff of a weapon of any kind, the person holding the weapon needs to end up in multiple pieces faster than it takes me to give the order.”

“Okay. Jesus. Dismember any threats. I’ll write that down.”

Jake took a moment to catch his breath, but when he spoke again, the exhaustion of the run was clearly audible. Jess flashed him a concerned look that he pointedly ignored. “What else?”

Jess pursed her lips together. “Well, the only other possibility is… internal.”

They fell silent for a moment. During the recent terrorist encounter in France, it came to light that a mole in the Secret Service was working with Trident, the terrorist organization responsible for the multiple assassination attempts on the President. Jake had enlisted the help of his friend and mentor, Max Harrison, to try to find the mole. Max had narrowed it down to two agents, but an internal investigation into both agents had proved inconclusive. Both of them were on unpaid leave and barred from contact with anyone in the agency and from access to the building, but the possibility that Max had gotten it wrong or that Trident would just turn another agent lingered.

“Has Art vetted the agents assigned to this mission?” Jake asked.

Art Davis was a Deputy Director of the Secret Service in charge of the President’s personal security. He and Jake were often at odds with each other, but Art’s loyalty wasn’t in question, and in this instance, both of them agreed that the traitor, when found, should face the harshest punishment the law allowed.

Maybe even a harsher punishment than that.

“He’s looked into all of them. Background, foreground, current ground, anything you can think of. He’s also interviewed them until they’ve cried.” Jake lifted an eyebrow, and she said, “Joking! Joking! No one cried, or if they did, I’m sure they were replaced. My point is that he did everything you would have done.”

Jake sighed. “Then we’ll just have to hope that’s enough.”

His legs began to shake, and he finally gave up on the rest of the run. He stopped and planted his hands on his knees, taking big, deep breaths that shuddered as he exhaled.

His side throbbed, and he must have shown that on his face because when Jess jogged back over to him, she had a frown on her face.

“Jake, seriously, I told you. You need to stop acting like some big macho man and give your body time to heal.”

“It’s had time to heal,” he said irritably.

“Stop acting like an idiot,” she snapped. “I mean it. If you ever want to be a big macho badass again, you need to *rest*. You shouldn’t even be coming on this damned trip.”

“We talked about that,” Jake said, straightening slowly. “I’m coming.”

“We talked about you not being an idiot and reinjuring yourself too. You don’t want to listen to me, so why should I listen to you?”

“Jess, I…” Jake’s voice trailed off when he saw Jess’s expression. Her normally bubbly face was tight with worry, and her eyes flashed with anger and fear. “All right,” he said softly. “I’ll be more careful.”

“You’re lying,” she said. It wasn’t a question.

He sighed and lifted his hands, letting them drop to his sides. “I’ll do my best, okay?”

It was Jess's turn to sigh in exasperation. She crossed her arms and shook her head. "Air Force One takes off at eleven. That gives you four hours to go home, shower, and pack. They'll have coffee and food on the plane, but if you feel like eating, you can do that first too."

“Jess, I’ll try, okay? I’ll take care of myself.”

She met his eyes, and when she said, “Sure you will,” the sarcasm in her tone made it clear she didn’t believe him.

He didn’t bother to argue further. He knew he wouldn’t take it as easy as she wanted. He didn’t care if it hurt, he *couldn’t* just sit and do nothing while Trident still operated.

She held his gaze for a minute or two before her eyes softened. “Sometimes I really hate you,” she said.

“Yeah. I know.”

She turned and continued her run without another word. Jake stood where he was until the pain in his side subsided enough that he could walk. Then he went home.

CHAPTER TWO

It probably shouldn't have surprised Jake that his unease didn't dissipate at all during the flight. Air Force One was a comfortable plane and, more importantly, as secure a location as possible. If there were one thing Jake knew, it was that on Air Force One, the president was safe. Usually, that allowed him to calm down a bit and enjoy a moment of respite from the constant stress of protecting the President.

It didn't work this time, and it got worse when the plane touched down. He wasn't happy about them going to Syria in the first place. The fact that there would be a public conference in an amphitheater right next to the airport angered him. Supposedly, it would make it easy for the President to escape if necessary, but it also made it easy for terrorists to get in and out.

As the plane taxied along the runway, he saw the amphitheater was even closer than he thought. Within walking distance.

"You okay?" Jess asked as the plane approached the gate.

"Doesn't matter," Jake asked. "The President has made it clear time and again that my concerns for his safety pale in comparison to his political need to wave his dick around."

Jess glanced around nervously, but none of the other agents seemed to notice. They did, of course, but they probably all agreed with Jake, and even if they didn't, it's not like anyone was going to tell the President how they felt.

They made it to the amphitheater without incident, which should have relieved Jake somewhat, but didn't. The amphitheater was a sniper's playground, an easy target for bombs both personal and dropped by aircraft, a nice barrel for terrorists to shoot the President in as though he were a fish and generally a goddamned security nightmare. Jake realized that it wasn't possible for the President to run the country from an underground nuclear bunker with a brigade of Secret Service agents to protect him, but that didn't mean he had to be happy about it.

And the amphitheater was filled with press. Too many to control effectively with the limited number of Secret Service they had. The wall of bodyguards Jake wanted was not nearly enough of a wall to protect from a myriad of threats.

Why was there so much press? It was an unusually large number of photographers, an unusually large number of reporters. There was more press here than if they were at a political rally stateside.

"There's too damned many people here," Jake groused.

From beside him, Jess said, "Well, maybe it will make it better if I tell you that any of those news drones could actually be weaponized so there could also be a massacre."

He glared at her, and she lifted her hands. "Jesus, it's just a joke."

He looked away, and she said, "This is the part where you say something like, 'I'm not Jesus, I'm Jake.'"

"Can it be the part where I tell you that you're being annoying and not funny?"

"Sure. You should know that only makes me want to tease you more, though."

He sighed, but against his will, he found himself smiling.

"Aww, there's that cute little smile."

"Please don't call me cute."

"Too late!"

He looked around and saw she was right. There were a great number of drones, and any of them could be weaponized. There was no way to tell from this distance.

"Does the Air Force not have top cover?" he asked.

"No. Like I said, it's a big ask to have the U.S. military control airspace and ground space in a foreign country."

"And I said I don't give a shit," Jake snapped. "I'm done letting other people be responsible for the President's security."

"Okay," Jess said mildly. "Feel free to tell that to the President, the Secretary of Defense, the Chiefs of Staff, the unit commanders in the area, and a number of other people ranked far more highly than you or I. That's only the American officials too."

"All right, you've made your point," he grumbled. He shook his head. "Back home, we would be able to just keep him on the plane."

"Welcome to Syria," she said with an exaggerated smile.

The President joined them a moment later. He nodded curtly at Jake but offered no other greeting. Jake wasn't sure if that was because he was maintaining a professional demeanor or because of the tension between them ever since Jake started dating his daughter. The two men had once been friends, but once it came out that Jake was in a relationship with Sheila, the President had barely spoken to him.

At least Sheila and her mother would remain on Air Force One during the conference. That was a silver lining.

He and Sheila hadn't spoken on the flight. If the President was ambivalent about Jake's relationship with his daughter, the First Lady actively hated it. She sat next to Sheila and made sure to shoot as many daggers out of her eyes at Jake as she possibly could.

Jake was all right with that. He and Sheila had enough time together stateside. Besides, his attention needed to be focused on the upcoming event, not on his romance with the President's daughter.

Jake walked with Jess in front of the president as they made their way to the amphitheater. There was no way he would have been allowed to speak in this place if Jake had any advanced knowledge of the venue. It had no good vantage points. If Jake had wanted to design a location that made it easy to kill a politician, he couldn't have done a better job than whoever designed this place.

Jess pointed upward. He looked up and saw helicopters. Jess said, "Now, they can have drones actually designed for military purposes and not just weaponized hobby drones."

"Remind me again why I invite you places," he grumbled.

"It's my exciting personality," she replied. "My bright and cheerful disposition." When Jake didn't laugh or smile this time, she rolled her eyes. "I'll talk to the Air Force. They might be able to scramble some jets to patrol over northern Israel within range of the helicopters. I don't know if it would help to shoot them down directly over the President, but if it'll make you relax, I'll try it."

He glanced up again. There were at least seven press helicopters. "Do you have field glasses with you?" he asked.

"I have supervision," she said, "didn't you know?"

He glared at her again, and she rolled her eyes. "God. Yes, I have field glasses. I'm trying to cheer you up."

"That's a waste of time," Jake said. He sighed. "I'm sorry, Jess. I'm just not going to be happy until this bullshit conference is over with, and we can take the President home."

"I know," she said. "Just try not to assume the worst. Remember that the President was perfectly safe for three years before Trident tried to kill him."

"Well, that was then. This is… hold on."

"What?"

Jake lifted his hand, and the agents behind him immediately grabbed the President. The President sighed irritably, but Jake couldn't give a rat's ass about Bryan's irritation level at the moment.

The drones were moving, forming a tight circle directly over them. Warning bells flashed in Jake's mind.

He turned and threw himself at the President just before a streak of light arced down from one of the drones, burning a hole into the ground directly where the President was standing only a moment ago.

"Move"! he shouted, yanking the President to his feet and pushing him toward the exit.

Thankfully, Bryan allowed Jake to move him without protest. The other agents instantly formed a protective shield around him. The drones fired again, and the searing light burned through the clothing of one agent and began to sear his arm. The man—an agent Jake recognized as Harkness, the leader of the President's personal security detail—cried out as his flesh began to bubble, but he kept his arm over the President, and a moment later, the laser or heat beam or whatever it was winked out.

Next to Jake, Jess was quickly tapping commands into her phone. Jake looked up to see the drones firing again, but this time, the beams moved in random directions, striking locations all across the amphitheater. Jake heard press agents screaming and saw them running in all directions as people realized the location was under attack.

"That'll keep the drones occupied for a while," Jess said. "It should give us enough time to get to safety."

Jake led the President toward the airport, but when he saw a dozen more drones arrayed around Air Force One, he tapped his earpiece and switched to plan B. "Get the chicks out of the nest ASAP. The drake awaits a raft."

"Roger that," Special Agent Miranda Stevens, the transportation coordinator, replied. "Raft is inbound."

Jess tapped more controls on her watch, and the drones around Air Force One began to veer wildly. Several crashed—into the ground, into Air Force One, into each other—and the others flew in shaky patterns in random directions. Jake glanced at the airplane and saw several scorch marks from the drone attacks, but the jet appeared flyable.

He couldn't risk that it wasn't, though. He wasn't a pilot or aircraft mechanic, and he had no way of knowing if the drones had fried something and rendered the plane unflyable. He couldn't risk putting the President on the plane or allowing his family to remain onboard.

A moment later, five armored SUVs pulled up. Three of the SUVs were armed with heavy machine guns, one with an RPG launcher and one with a powerful EM jammer. Special Forces operators—Delta Force, Jake guessed, or SOG—hopped out of the vehicles and opened side doors.

Harkness broke away and headed to one of the vehicles armed with a machine gun. It doubled as their medical vehicle. Jake made a mental note to visit him later and commend him for his service.

He, Jess, the President, and two members of the President's personal security detail entered the vehicle armed with an EM jammer. The other Secret Service agents entered the other three vehicles.

The SUVs sped off, heading toward the safehouse the CIA had arranged in case of exactly what had happened. The whole event from the drone attack to the evacuation took three minutes.

It was an excellent extraction, but as Jake looked out the rear window of the SUV to five more armored vehicles leaving Air Force One, he couldn't bring himself to feel good. Once more, they were stuck in a foreign country under threat of an assassination attempt on the President's life.

CHAPTER THREE

"I'll handle damage control," Jake said, "but first and foremost, let me secure you and secure your family. Once we've done that, I can work with local authorities until we get you back on your way to Washington."

"I'm not going to Washington," the President replied, "I have a job to do here."

Jake had to take a moment to remember he was standing in the Oval Office speaking with the Leader of the Free World, the President of the United States, and the final decision maker for just about everything, and not his friend Bryan Jackson.

It was better to remember that than to raise his voice. He still couldn't eliminate all of his anger as he said, "Please tell me that's a joke. Please, Mr. President, tell me you're not foolish enough to remain here."

Only a trace of anger flashed behind Bryan's eyes before he smiled and said, "I don't think I'd let anyone else get away with talking to me like that Jake. I'm staying in Syria. That's non-negotiable. Next topic?"

Jake sighed and nodded. "We'll get your family home, then. I'm going to arrange security for…"

"My family is staying with me, Jake." He lifted a hand to cut Jake off before he could say anything. "I know how you feel about it, but we're not going to let terrorists determine my schedule. We're not going to be pushed around by them. It's not going to happen."

Jake took a breath and managed to control his tone as he asked, "Non-negotiable?"

"Non-negotiable."

Jake sighed. He took a moment to stop himself from asking why the President felt that making everyone aware of the size of his balls was more important than Sheila's safety. When he got himself under control, he nodded. "Okay. In that case, the first order of business is for me to secure you and your family here. We'll determine the next steps afterward. I'm going to check with Jess, with Agent Foster, and see what she's learned. I need to call Director Davis, too. I can't promise he'll accept non-negotiable."

The President smiled. "Well, you don't accept it, Jake. It's still happening, though."

Jake's lips thinned, but he kept his tone professional. "Sir, with all due respect to you both as the President and my friend, you and your family *will* be leaving Syria as soon as Air Force One is deemed flyable. My sources tell me that will take roughly twenty-four hours. You have exactly that long to do whatever job you think you need to do. After that, you will be on that airplane. You can feel free to imprison me when you get home, but France *will not* happen again."

Before the President could react, Jake nodded and said, "I'll be back shortly, Sir."

The two agents assigned to the President's personal protection returned to his side. The safehouse was located on the airport, an underground facility the CIA had constructed during the Syrian Civil War when it was believed that the Syrian president had access to nuclear weapons. When the time came to leave the country, they would be seconds away from Air Force One.

At the moment, Air Force One sat in a hangar just above the safehouse. Jake headed to the plane and found Jess inside, huddled over her laptop.

"Let me guess," she said without looking up, "we don't let terrorists decide the schedule."

"Not even for his family," Jake said bitterly. "I told him he has until this plane is deemed flyable to do whatever he has to do. Then we drag him onboard kicking and screaming, and I accept my prison sentence after we get him safely home."

Jess's lips thinned slightly. Jake understood. His relationship with Sheila was inappropriate for many reasons, and this only made that clear. It wasn't his job to tell the President what to do, but he had done just that. It was no wonder Jess didn't approve.

She knew better than to argue with him about it, though. "Well, I'm sifting through footage," she said. "The amphitheater and nearby areas. Ideally, I'll come up with some clues about the attack we can use to determine who launched it."

"And its point of origin," he said.

"It's point of origin?" Jess said. "Why in the world would I want to determine its point of origin? Doesn't it make more sense just to analyze what happened without worrying about how to find the people who did it?"

"Seriously, Jess," he said, "I'm in no mood."

“Yeah, well I’m in the mood, so deal with it,” she replied. She turned his way but lifted her eyebrows, looking behind him.

He turned around. General Hawks stood there, a bitter expression on his face. “I’m sure you know how important this situation is,” he said.

Under ordinary circumstances, Jake might have been offended at Hawks’ veiled questioning of Jake’s abilities. At the moment, however, he was too busy being pissed off at the President to be upset at the Secretary of Defense right now, so he only said, “Yes, Sir.”

“I think it’s related to the attack at the bunker,” the Secretary replied.

Last week, an international arms dealer had attacked a bunker so secret that even Jake didn’t know where it was. The only fatality was a senatorial aide who had been pierced by a flagpole dislodged when the terrorists detonated a bomb to break into the bunker, but it was suspected that the terrorists stole a number of plans for top-secret Pentagon weapons research.

“Hadad?” Jake asked.

Hadad was an international arms dealer who had run afoul of the United States after he was caught arming insurgents fighting American forces in the Middle East.

It was an interesting theory. It was also a plausible theory. If nothing else, it would explain the energy weapons the drones used in the attack earlier today.

The general nodded, and Jake said, “Agent Foster is examining footage of the attacks and analyzing footage from the surrounding area as well. We’re hoping we’ll get some evidence of the origins.”

Hawks stepped forward and soon the three of them were fully engaged in a conversation while examining screenshots, recorded, and live footage. It was Hawks who said, “You don’t have the power here.”

Jake thought for a moment he was correcting her, pointing out a lack of authority or something. Jess, however, said, "No. No, I don't." She turned to Jake and said, "I need to get back to Washington. If I'm going to get anything out of this footage, I need better tech."

“Better tech than we have on Air Force One?”

Hawks replied to that. “Air Force One is crammed full of countermeasures to any kind of electromagnetic assault you can think of, but it doesn’t have the capability to analyze data. It’s designed to keep the President safe and facilitate his interaction with the nation’s security apparatus, but it's not designed to analyze evidence and draw conclusions."

Jake sighed. "I don't suppose you can tell me that the only way back is on Air Force One, and the President will just have to go home after all?"

Jess gasped and looked nervously at Hawks, but the Secretary didn't seem offended or appalled by Jake's statement. On the contrary, he replied, "No, I'm afraid not. The Air Force is still going over everything to make sure the jet won't crash into the ocean on its way home. We'll be sending Special Agent Foster home on a private transport."

Jake nodded. "All right. Well, in the meantime, I'm going to head back to the safehouse and ensure that the President and his family are as safe as possible. Sir?" he said to Hawks, "Will you be staying here or returning home?"

"I will be returning with Special Agent Foster," Hawks replied. "We need to look into the possibility that the Syrian government had something to do with this attack, and I'd rather the Department of Defense handle that. People tend to stop posturing when I talk to them, so I'm going to go back home to make sure things proceed smoothly."

"Understood, sir."

"Keep your chin up, Mercer," the Secretary said unexpectedly. "You're doing a good job. You face an unprecedented threat in Trident, and you've successfully kept the President safe despite that challenge. You should be proud."

Jake smiled. "I'd rather the President was safe, but pending that, sir, I'll take pride."

Hawks laughed, and Jake wondered if he was the first person to ever hear that sound from the notoriously taciturn General. "Every silver lining we can get, right Marine?"

"Yes, sir."

Jake left a surprised Jess and an unusually jovial Hawks and returned to the safehouse. The President was in a conference room on the phone with the Syrian President along with the leaders of Israel, Jordan, Lebanon, and Saudi Arabia discussing security in the region.

What an appropriate topic.

Jake met with his team leaders and ensured that appropriate security measures were in place. The hangar was locked down and protected by American servicemen over the protests of the Syrian President, who insisted they were embarrassing his country, a fact about which Jake couldn't care less. The safehouse was literally crawling with Secret Service agents. Jake didn't like being in Syria, but if he was forced to stay here, this was as safe a circumstance as he could hope for.

Of course, that didn't help them in France.

***

The Air Force was going over a few anomalies with Air Force One, but they assured him the jet would be ready to take off soon. The President managed to get enough work done that he wasn't particularly pissy about needing to leave as soon as the jet was ready. Sheila was very intentionally kept apart from Jake by her mother, but that was still all right with Jake. They'd be home soon enough, and then it wouldn't matter how the First Lady felt about them.

The next morning, Jess called Jake. "I have something."

"Go ahead."

"So the drones were controlled by a unique software that could operate all of the drones independently while still coordinating attacks on specific targets. It operates similarly to a greatly simplified version of our own military's Link 16."

"Do we know who developed it?"

"That's the something. I don't know who developed it, but I traced the software back to a tech sector in Amman, Jordan."

"Jordan has a tech sector?"

"I guess so. Either way, the code was scripted in a programming language used by Jordanian Arabic speakers, and there are a couple of software markers that point to its origins in Amman."

"Got it. Thank you."

"I don't suppose I can convince you to let the CIA handle the investigation part?"

"I don't either."

Jess didn't say anything for a moment. Then she sighed. "Can I at least convince you to remember you're injured and not get yourself killed?"

Jake felt a pang in his midsection as though his own body were trying to remind him of the truth of what Jess was saying. "Yes," he replied. "You can convince me of that much."

"Good. I don't want to see you get hurt."

"I'll do my best."

Jess sighed. "Good luck, Jake."

CHAPTER FOUR

It came later than he wanted it to come. When Jake watched Air Force One rise into the air, though, it was difficult to be angry at how long it took. What was important was that he finally got the President to agree to return to DC. Better yet, Hawks took the President's safety as seriously as Jake did. There was an aircraft carrier very close by, and the Air Force had a squadron of stealth fighters ready to scramble. Air Force One would make it to DC unmolested. Still until Jake received confirmation of that fact, he wouldn't be able to relax at all.

He probably wouldn't be able to relax even after Air Force One landed in Washington. Jake wanted the President to cancel the Middle East Tour. Hell, anyone with a brain wanted him to scuttle the trip. Instead, in his typical bullheadedness, he made it clear that he intended to complete the other legs of his itinerary on schedule. He would be back, and Jake couldn't do a damned thing to change that. The President was leaving now, though. Sheila was leaving now, and that was good.

He waited until Air Force One was no longer visible before heading into the terminal to find his gate. The flight from Damascus to Amman took six and a half hours, including transfer time. He had a great deal of information to review in order to fill that time.

By the time the flight landed, he wondered why Hadad was still alive.

It seemed bizarre to him that they allowed men like Hadad to build organizations. They spent plenty of resources taking out far less dangerous people. He'd participated in such missions as a Marine. If Hadad were really to blame for the attack in Damascus, it felt to Jake like General Hawks' fault.

No. It felt like the fault of whatever department would make the decision to take Hadad out. It could have been done back when that was a relatively easy thing to do. Now, Hadad knew he was a target. This was true because of the bunker attack. Regardless of the attack in Syria, he knew he was a target. That in itself made the mission more difficult. The fact that he had access not only to black-market tech but possibly to American military tech complicated things further.

As he disembarked and arranged for lodging, he formulated a plan. He wouldn't be able to track Hadad in the endless sea of faces here in Jordan. However, he could track the technology. "You have an exceptional understanding of urban landscapes, remember," he said into the water. That was an assessment from Art. He'd mentioned it when he first started, and after the events in Paris of a few months ago, Jake finally understood what Art meant and how that skill could help him.

He might not, of course, be able to get to any drone software directly, but he could get to where the technology was bought and sold. His first step was to find such a place.

The best places to look for advanced technology were, ironically, places that sold cheap or vintage tech. While anything visible at such a place would be bargain basement parts intended for kids building cheap computers in their basements, the people who frequented and operated such establishments were people who worshipped technology and were no doubt aware of the latest and greatest in tech of any kind. It was no guarantee that any of them would have black market connections, but it was the first place to look.

Jess's voice came over his earpiece as he stepped out of his safehouse onto the bustling city streets. "I have some candy," she said.

"Candy" in this case was information that could prove helpful or even decisive to his mission.

"How sweet is it?" he asked.

"Super sweet. Sweeter than a kiss from Sheila."

"I doubt that," Jake replied, "but I'll take it. What do you have?"

"Check your phone."

Jake did, and what he saw was indeed sweet. It was an image of the attack on the bunker. Specifically, it was an image of one of the people implicated in the attack. "Who am I looking at?"

"That, my good sir, is Fahad Al-Azir. He's one of Hadad's most well-known associates. He was spotted in Amman last week. No idea if he's still there, but if you happen to run into him, that'll make your life easier."

"Yes, it will," Jake agreed. "Thank you."

"You're most welcome."

Jake walked through the markets and eventually made his way to the first of the tech shops. He was immediately approached by a grinning man who recognized him as American and assumed that meant he had a lot of money and very little sense. Unfortunately for him, Jake wasn't here to spend that money, so after ten minutes of haggling, he had to content himself with charging Jake twenty dollars for a five-dollar flash drive that Jake was fairly sure wouldn't work.

The next three shops ended in similar results. Jake looked through each shop for a sign of anything that might indicate involvement in black-market sales and from time to time talked with people and dropped hints that he was a "serious buyer" looking for something serious.

That only resulted in desperate attempts by shopkeepers to sell Jake last-generation gaming computers with long lists of dubious upgrades for outrageous prices. Jake was about ready to give up and try another tack, but in the fifth shop he visited, he heard a voice behind him when he mentioned he was a serious buyer.

"If you're a serious buyer," the voice said, "then you need to buy from a serious seller."

Jake turned toward the voice and found himself face to face with Fahad Al-Azir. Before he had a chance to talk to him, though, Fahad's smile vanished. He paled, and just before Jake could react, he turned and ran. Jake rushed after him, pushing past surprised shopkeepers and buyers and rushing into the street. For a terrifying moment, he lost Fawad, but then he caught the terrorist heading toward an alleyway on the opposite side of the street.

How the hell had he recognized Jake? What kind of intelligence did Hadad have?

Jake sprinted after him, tapping his earpiece. "Jess, I'm pursuing Al-Azir."

"Wait, you found him?"

"Yes. He was in one of the tech shops. I posed as someone looking for weapons, and he started trying to sell to me. He's on foot, moving through the alleyways."

As he spoke, he saw Fahad turn down a side alley. "I don't suppose you have eyes here?" he asked Jess.

"Not in Jordan, no. I can see what you see, but you're putting yourself at—"

Jake turned down the same alley as Fahad and saw the man sprinting with admirable speed and endurance toward a brick wall.

"Risk," Jess finished. "Jake, you're not fully healed. You promised me you'd remember that."

"I'm fine," Jake said. "I can't lose him. We have a chance to nip this one in the bud, and I need to take that chance."

"Jake, come on," Jess said. "Don't get yourself hurt. You can't help anyone if you're dead."

Fahad vaulted over the brick wall just as Jake reached it. He climbed after Fahad, grimacing a little as his abdomen started to throb.

"Jake, if it hurts, promise me you'll stop," Jess said. When he didn't answer, she insisted, "Jake!"

“I need to bring him in for questioning,” Jake said. “I can’t just let him get away. If you want me to stop, then you need to help me.”

“How can I help you? I don’t have any resources.”

“Right,” Jake said, veering down another alley as Fahad turned left. “I don’t suppose you have an up-to-date map of the city’s alleyways?”

“I can get one, but it’s not going to help since all I can see is the backsides of buildings.”

“Pull it up anyway. If this chase makes it back to city streets, I can tell you where I am, and you can help me head him off.”

“Or, and just hear me out, you can admit that you lost him and then keep yourself safe.”

“Jess, we’re not having this argument again.”

Fahad looked behind to see if he had shaken Jake. When he found the Secret Service Agent still hot on his heels, he shines and lowered his head, quickening his pace. Jake sped up as well, and the ache in his midsection became a throb.

Of greater concern was the fact that he was already breathing heavily. Months spent convalescing had weakened his cardio, and lingering complications from the virus he had been infected with in France had sapped his endurance. He wasn’t sure how much longer he would be able to keep up this pace.

He needed to catch Fahad quickly.

The terrorist looked over his shoulder, and when he saw that Jake was still following closely, he looked around for a different escape route. His eyes fixed on a hanging fire escape, and Jake’s heart sank.

Please don’t climb the damned roof, he thought silently.

In Paris, before being infected with the virus, Jake had chased a man he later learned was none other than Vincent St. Clair, the creator of the virus, across rooftops and a train yard. It wasn’t an experience he cared to repeat, and definitely not one he cared to repeat in his condition.

As though on cue, a stabbing pain shot through his stomach. He winced, and Jess must have noticed from the change in her perspective what had happened. “Are you okay? Jake, call it off!”

If Fahad had taken the fire escape, Jake might have listened. He didn't think he could jump across rooftops without seriously reinjuring himself.

But the terrorist thought better of it and instead ran out of another alley into a busy street. Jake followed and found the man trying to lose himself in a crowd.

Jake made a show of looking around as though he had lost Fahad before running across the street to the opposite alley. He counted to five, then walked back out into the crowd of people. A quick scan showed Fahad looking behind him, searching for Jake. Jake kept his head down and his hands in his pockets, and after a moment, Fahad sighed with relief and turned ahead.

Jake kept following slowly, keeping his eyes fixed on Fahad but making sure that he didn't appear to be looking at or following the man.

Fahad left the crowded downtown and turned down a side street. Jake followed, but as the crowd thinned, it became clear that he wasn't going to be able to hide himself much longer.

So, when the crowd thinned enough that he couldn't hide among it, he sprinted toward Fahad. The terrorist heard his footsteps a moment too late. He turned, shrieked and started to run from Jake, but Jake caught him before he could run.

"Let me go!" he cried in English. "Let me go!

He tried to struggle, but he was clearly not a fighter, and even weakened, Jake had no trouble dragging him to an alley. He threw him down to the ground and planted a foot in his chest.

"Move and die," he said, a threat he didn't plan to carry out, obviously, but one that had the desired effect of scaring Fahad into silence.

Jake called Jess and when she answered, she said, "I kind of wish he had kicked your ass for being so irresponsible."

"Sorry to disappoint." He looked around. "Okay, did you see the street signs?"

"Yes, I saw them."

"Okay. I need a place where I can talk to Fahad. Preferably somewhere we won't be interrupted."

"I have just the place."

Jake grinned at Fahad and yanked him to his feet. "All right, let's go talk."

CHAPTER FIVE

Jake felt a little silly. He couldn't deny the situation was cliché. It was, in fact, very likely the most cliché situation possible. Dark room. Single light bulb hanging from the ceiling and swaying to the breeze of a fan hidden in the darkness. The scene couldn't be designed better by a world-class cinematographer.

Actually, it probably could be designed much better. Almost certainly any review for this movie, if it were ever made a movie, would be about how utterly ridiculous this particular scene was. If the positions were reversed, this would read very comically. The hero would make wisecracks while the menacing interrogator would get angrier and angrier. Then, either the hero would be knocked out, and the scene would cut to him waking up in a cell, or an unlikely but exciting burst of violence would result in the death of the interrogator and Jake's freedom.

But it was the best Jake could do. He wasn't a trained interrogator. A better way to put that was that Jake wasn't trained in enhanced interrogation techniques.

But he'd find a way. Just as he had in Paris interrogating Hans, who would later be revealed as none other than Vincent St. Clair, the mastermind behind the virus that had killed thousands of French people and nearly Jake himself, he would find a way to get the answers he needed.

Jake wouldn't have had a moral problem with the course of action, but he doubted it would be effective on someone like Fahad. Fahad was already weeping and shaking violently. If Jake harmed him in any way, even superficially, he'd probably wilt into a blubbering mess and become completely useless. He needed to find a way to get answers without violence.

Jess spoke over the earpiece. "Have you started talking to him yet?"

"Wouldn't you hear if I did?"

"Well, I would now, but I wasn't paying attention earlier. Once I determined that you weren't going to get yourself killed, I started looking into Fahad to see if I could link him to anything that might help us."

"And you have something?"

"Well, I've learned that he's an idiot. At least if his goal is to avoid discovery."

"How do you mean?"

"Well, I haven't finished the discovery process, but I've found a trail of electronic funds transfers. A lot of money seems to have moved through Fahad's hands before disappearing to various accounts in Jordan, Iran, Iraq, and Qatar. So far, the two accounts in Jordan are zero-balance accounts. Money arrives and leaves instantly. That's how they all should have been set up. Fahad is either too inexperienced to know that or too arrogant to care."

"What does that mean for us?"

"Well, one possibility is that he isn't a very valuable asset. He could be nothing more than a foot-soldier for Hadad."

"A foot-soldier given responsibility over money?"

"Responsibility is the wrong word. A better word would be patsy."

"How do we know for sure?"

"First and foremost, we dig deeper into the transactions. Well, *I* do. We need to know where the money's coming from. That's more important than determining where the money goes. We know that it ultimately ends up in Hadad's hand, but I want to figure out who Hadad's sources are."

"So what do you need from me?"

"You need to get Fahad to tell you everyone Hadad is buying tech from and selling tech to. You need to figure out what Hadad's plan is for the President, and while you're at it, maybe find out if our buddies from Trident are involved."

"They're involved. I'm sure of that."

"Me too, but we need to know beyond a shadow of a doubt. Also, finding out where the money is coming from might tell us where Bard and Drew are now."

Jake's lips thinned at the mention of the Trident leaders' names. Eli Bard was a former Secret Service agent renowned as one of the best the Service had ever produced. Even after he had been rather ignominiously canned for his extreme political views, he was still spoken of in the Service with the same reverence with which the FBI spoke of Elliot Ness and his Untouchables.

At least until it was revealed that he was a nutjob who didn't mind killing civilians indiscriminately to get to the President and the other members of the Cabinet.

More painful than Bard's terrorist activities, however, was the other man. Drew, full name Andrew McNeill, was a former Marine and Jake's erstwhile best friend. That friendship had ended abruptly when an op botched due to an unforeseen ambush had resulted in the deaths of six Navy SEALs and the dishonorable discharge of McNeill from the Marine Corps.

Jake knew Drew was bitter, but when he learned that Drew was Bard's second in command in Trident, he was crushed. He would never have predicted that Drew would betray his country to this degree. He'd even shot at Jake in Paris.

"All right," Jake said. "I'll talk to him and see what I can find out."

"*Talk* to him, Jake. Keep in mind that St. Clair lied to us in spite of what you did to him."

Jake stiffened but forced himself to remain calm. "I'll start that way, Jess. That's the most I can promise. Like you said, we need this information."

Jess didn't answer for a few beats. When she did, she simply said, "All right."

Jake sighed and focused on the task at hand. He headed to the room where Fahad waited, shivering with fear. He pulled up the only other chair in the room and sat. If this were a movie, he would sit so that his face was hidden in shadow, but instead, he sat in a way that left his face clearly visible.

It had the effect he intended. Fahad's eyes fixed on him, and when he saw the deadly seriousness in Jake's expression, his eyes widened, and a soft whimper escaped his lips.

"Did you hear what I was saying to my friend?" he asked.

Fahad shook his head.

"This will be your only warning of any kind," Jake told him. "When I ask a question, I expect you to answer with words. Do you understand?"

Fahad nodded. Jake started to rise from his chair, and the terrorist quickly said, "Yes! Yes, I understand!"

Jake sat back down. "Wonderful. What is your name?"

"Mahmoud Kazmir."

Jake frowned. "Not Fahad Al-Azir?"

The man shook his head. "We use fake names when we work with Hadad. He insists on it. That way no one can betray anyone else, even if…"

"Even if what?"

The man—Mahmoud or Fahad or whatever his name was—closed his eyes and whispered, “Please.”

Jake started to rise, and the man whimpered, “Even if we’re tortured for information. Please listen, I was just a buyer for him. I didn’t hurt anyone.”

Jake shook his head. “Mm, see, that’s a lie. I’m going to tell you how I know it’s a lie, but first, I’m going to punish you.”

"No! Please! I… I… the bunker, right? You know, because someone took a picture of me at the bunker?"

“How do you know about that picture?”

“I… I just guessed. You’re American, and that’s the only time I’ve been to America, so it had to be there.”

Jake bought that answer. It was plausible. He also believed that Mahmoud would tell him the truth. He was at best delusional if he truly considered himself innocent, but he was clearly terrified for his life. He would get every bit of information Mahmoud had. Depending on how frightened the man was of Hadad, Jake might have to be a little persuasive in his pursuit of the information, but Mahmoud would eventually tell everything he knew.

“Okay. I believe you.”

Mahmoud slumped forward with relief. “Thank you,” he said, his voice thready.

“So,” Jake said. “What did you buy for Hadad?”

“Whatever he needed. It didn’t matter. Sometimes technology—wires and switches and stuff for detonators and things like that.”

“Not advanced drone parts?”

Mahmoud shook his head. “No. I don’t know where he got that weaponry.”

“So it *was* you at the conference in Syria.”

“No! Not me!”

Jake made a circular motion with his finger. “You plural. You guys. Hadad and Trident.”

At the mention of Trident, the man’s eyes snapped forward. Jake smiled. “So you know Trident. Ever met Eli Bard?”

“No. I know Trident is the person paying Hadad to attack the President, but I don’t know who Eli Bard is. Is he Trident?”

“What about Andrew McNeill?” Jake asked, ignoring Mahmoud’s question.

"I don't know him. Is he Trident, too? Listen, I just handle the money."

"Uh huh." Jake shifted forward slightly in his chair. Mahmoud flinched and closed his eyes, anticipating a blow. That told Jake he knew he had been caught in a lie. "So we started with you telling me that you just bought things for Hadad. Now you're saying you handle the money. Not some money, not a little bit of money, *the* money. All the money. That makes you his treasurer. That's a little bit more important than just a buyer."

Mahmoud lowered his head. He shook like a leaf.

"Where is Hadad right now?"

"I don't know," Mahmoud said, his voice barely a whisper. "After we raided the bunker, it was agreed that we should split up. I came here. I don't know where the others went."

"Who are the others?"

Mahmoud swallowed. "There is me, Hadad, Angel, Ishmael, Edom and Abdul. All fake names."

"And you never heard anyone talk about where they lived? Where they grew up? What kind of home they lived in?"

"No. We knew better. We knew that one day, one of us would end up here. We knew… We know that when we are caught, it is over for us. We will be tortured for information and then killed. Our bodies will be defiled, and we will never see our families again."

His eyes snapped open when he said that. He looked at Jake in horror and pleaded, "Please don't hurt my family! They know *nothing* about what I do!"

"As long as you're honest with me, no one will get hurt," Jake said, choosing his words carefully. He had no desire to hurt Mahmoud's family, but it might be useful for Mahmoud to think that he would.

"Oh God," Mahmoud wailed. "I've told you what I know!"

"Calm down," Jake said gently, lifting a hand in a placating motion. "Relax. You're doing great, Mahmoud. You don't know where Hadad and his E Street Band are. That's okay. I believe you. It fits with what we know of Hadad. What about Trident? Do you know where *they* are? I know you don't know names, but do you know where the money came from? We've seen the transactions, and we know that Trident paid you to carry out these attacks. Any idea where that money came from?"

Mahmoud shook his head. "It was sent to us via distributed networks. Different currencies, different computers, different locations each time. Of course, it was all converted to U.S. dollars, so it won't show that way, but that's how we received it. Trident was very clear that they would help us only if we agreed not to find them."

Jake tried to hide his frustration. If he could have believed Mahmoud was lying, he wouldn't have been so upset, but the problem was he believed Mahmoud was telling the truth. Bard's schemes had shown varying levels of forethought, but the one thing he had managed to do every time was evade capture. It was clear that he took his personal safety seriously.

Jake wasn't sure what else he could learn from Mahmoud. Fortunately, Jess saved him from the need to learn anything else. "Jake, I found it. I traced the money back through the distributed networks he's talking about. Every payment came from an account based in Tikrit, Iraq."

Iraq? Jake frowned. First Syria, then Iraq. Bard was hiding in places that had recently had conflict with the United States. He might be hoping that people would follow the red herrings of those conflicts rather than focus on him and Hadad.

Well, he would learn the hard way that he was wrong to use that strategy.

"Please," Mahmoud said. Then, when Jake stood and approached him, "*Please!*" in a desperate shriek.

Jake leaned close to Mahmoud, so close their noses almost touched. In a quiet and deadly voice, he said. "I promise you, Mahmoud, if you ever come up in connection with Hadad, Trident or anything even tangentially related to an attack on the United States or any of its leaders, I will find you. I will take you somewhere the world doesn't even know exists, and I will take as long as I possibly can to kill you. Do you understand me?"

Mahmoud bought Jake's bluff hook, line and sinker. He shivered, swallowed and barely managed to say, "Yes."

"Good."

Jake turned to leave, and Mahmoud was so terrified, he didn't even ask Jake to remove his bonds.

Jake tapped his earpiece. "Jess, call someone to take Mahmoud into custody. I need a way into Tikrit, Iraq."

"Well, I have a way in, but you won't like it."

"What is it?"

Jess told him. When she finished, Jake swore. "Are you serious?"

"I told you you wouldn't like it."

"What the hell is he thinking? Is he trying to get himself assassinated?"

"I imagine not. I'm not brave like you, though. I didn't think it was a good idea to challenge the President's decision."

CHAPTER SIX

None of the bases in Iraq were more than FOBs, Forward Operating Bases. These were designed to support tactical, operational objectives in a secured location but had little of the logistics of a permanent military installation. Jake didn't feel comfortable with the situation. Not just the lack of resources, but the area in general. The political situation in Iraq was tenuous at best, and the President was in danger no matter where he was. He shouldn't be here, even if it was unannounced.

They were essentially makeshift fortresses on foreign soil. There were a few in the United States, of course, but those served different purposes. On foreign soil, they were established as a tactical necessity, but they weren't built with the safety features and security measures necessary for POTUS involvement. They served as intermediaries between supply lines and troops on the frontline. They were not designed for world leaders.

And they were vulnerable. Since they were somewhat more accessible than an actual permanent military base, they were targets for enemy forces, suicide bombers, snipers, and ideologues. More, too. The list was endless, and none of it boded well for the President.

Hell, the walls were lined with fucking sandbags instead of armor. The setup offered the illusion of fortress-like security, but it was just smoke and mirrors. Protecting the President required something real, not phantom strength.

The base would offer little beyond fundamental necessities. There would be no luxuries. There would simply be soldiers, some strong and some weak. Some hardened and some soft. Some would be fully committed to their missions. Some would be fully committed to surviving their deployment and getting home.

And they headed to such a place now, damn it. He was supposed to somehow protect the president.

He wished he knew who had given the President the idea that now would be a good time for a surprise visit to U.S. forces in the country. Art had assured him it was no one in the Secret Service. If it were, Jake would have been convinced that agent was working with Trident. As it was, he was at least half-sure that whatever agency they worked for, their loyalties lay with the President's enemies.

Not to mention the fact that it completely threw a wrench into Jake's plan to investigate the financial transactions in Tikrit. That problem, at least, was partially dealt with when Jess contacted a CIA connection of theirs known to them as Mr. Quartz and got him to agree to use assets in the area to dig up information. Jake would still have preferred to do the digging himself rather than use a contact in another agency whose mission was not solely the protection of the President and his family, but it was better than nothing.

For the love of God, what kind of morale boost would getting killed by a fucking roadside bomb provide? What was Jake supposed to do to ensure the President's safety? Sometimes, Jake thought Bryan had a death wish.

Maybe he's hoping that getting assassinated will cement his legacy, he thought irritably. That wasn't a kind thought to have, but there it was anyway.

Security in circumstances like that was all but impossible. He had soldiers with him, which was helpful-ish, but soldiers weren't trained to protect the President. They might be useful once they reached the Forward Operating Base, but what about during transport? In any situation, the President was at his most vulnerable when he was moving, and they were sitting ducks at the moment.

So Jake wasn't surprised to hear an explosive boom ten miles outside of the FOB nearest Tikrit. It was followed by the sickening crunch of metal-on-metal. He had about two seconds to think, *Yep. We're under attack. Because of course we are.*

Then the world exploded into chaos.

Jake's gaze snapped to the window, and he saw his worst fear come to life. A barrage of bullets tore through the convoy. Some broke through the armored vehicles like they were made of paper. Heavy machine guns. He looked up just in time to see a soldier's body jerk violently before collapsing onto the road. The warrior's blood stained the ground beneath him a dark red. Another crumpled where he stood. He couldn't hear anything over the gunfire, of course. It still seemed like he did. Jake still felt like he heard the thud of the second soldier's body.

Later, he would be angry at the President for causing these soldier's deaths because of his own pigheadedness. Right now, he had a job to do.

He leaped from his vehicle, immediately rolling on impact. He rolled forward and his ears hurt, no longer used to the noise of combat. The sound of the attack was deafening. Hollywood never got that part right. They focused on the gunfire. Occasionally, they caught the sound of a bullet splintering wood next to the hero's face. They never showed the constant, aggressive cacophony. There was constant ricochet. There was constant metallic chaos. Voices unending. It was even worse when you couldn't see. A few movies came close, especially the one about finding that one private in Germany after D-Day, but nothing truly resembled combat but combat.

He leapt up and sprinted towards the President's vehicle, kicking himself for choosing to be in the lead vehicle when the assault could come from any angle. The orchestra of violence and chaos didn't pause. In fact, it seemed to grow louder.

He saw a vehicle—not the President's—jump into the air, torn nearly in half by a high-caliber anti-material rifle, a 40-millimetre almost certainly. He could taste dust and blood in his mouth as he charged forward. It reminded him of things he didn't want to remember at all. The door to the President's vehicle was flung open just as he reached it. That wasn't protocol, but Jake didn't have time to lecture the soldier who opened the door on proper Secret Service extraction protocol.

The President fell from the car, and the soldier at least knew enough about protection to throw himself on top of him. Jake dove down, too. He and the guard got the President about twenty yards away before an explosion sent shredded pieces of the vehicle over their heads.

That one wasn't a rifle. That wasn't even an RPG. That was an honest to God rocket.

"Stay down, Mr. President!" he commanded.

Jake could rarely count on the President to comply when there was no immediate, evident danger. With the threat clear and present, though, Bryan didn't argue. The soldier said, "I'll cover you!" turned around, and started firing indiscriminately toward the horizon. Jake didn't know how helpful that would be, but he would take anything he could get.

Jake led the President to a shallow depression on the side of the road. He expected attackers or mines of some sort, but enjoyed a welcome stroke of luck when the dip was free of enemies. He threw the President to the ground and dove on top of him, pulling his handgun. He would have given his left leg for his rifle now. He hadn't used his sniper rifle in combat in over a decade, but he practiced regularly, and he was still a crack shot out to eight hundred yards.

The handgun had a range of fifty yards at best. If the wind was calm, Jake might have been able to push that to seventy-five, but a fresh breeze was blowing, and with the dust swirling the way it was, Jake would be lucky to place an accurate shot past thirty yards.

He would have to hope it didn't get to that point.

Then, the terrorists made a crucial mistake. Buoyed by their initial success, they revealed themselves, rising from cover just beyond a hill five hundred yards from Jake. A disorganized militia may have been too overwhelmed by the deadly surprise attack to react properly to the charging enemy, but the well-trained and combat-proven soldiers of the United States Army recognized their chance to extricate themselves from a bad position. The enemy's fired wildly, but even if they had fired with precision, their poorly maintained cheap copies of even cheaper Cold War era Russian weapons would have had a poor chance of reaching their targets at best. The soldiers maintained calm under fire, and as the enemy drew closer, Jake said, "Wait until they're within one hundred yards. Keep cover, and on my mark, we fire."

"Roger that," the captain in charge of the escort replied.

Jake waited for the enemy to close the distance. The President shifted his weight, and Jake said, "Stay still, sir."

Bryan stilled, and Jake silently counted down the seconds until the enemy was in range. Five… four… three… two… one…

"Mark!" Jake called.

The volley of fire unleashed by the soldiers was devastating. Fully a third of the one hundred-odd assailants fell dead. The others quickly separated, half of them stopping and staring in confusion, and half of them continuing toward the Americans without entirely realizing what had happened.

They realized it the second volley, those few who remained alive anyway. They began to turn tail and run, but as far as Jake could see, none of them escaped. When the situation was under control, Jake radioed the captain. "Is there a vehicle available to transport the President?"

"The Bradleys are all right," the captain replied. "You can take one of them, and I'll send Lieutenant Pressley in another to escort you back to the reservation. I'll stay here to guard the bodies of my fallen soldiers until we can be extracted."

Jake felt a pang for the captain. He knew what it was like to lose men under his command. He hated that he had to leave. The Marine in him screamed that he should stand stalwart with the captain until all of his men were evacuated, but he had a responsibility to the President, and clearly, Bryan's surprise visit was no longer a surprise.

"All right. Thank you, sir."

"It's the job, Marine," the captain replied in a voice tinged with grief and resignation. "You know it as well as I do."

That was the captain's way of tacitly acknowledging that he understood that Jake needed to leave. Jake noted he referred to Jake as a Marine and not as an agent. That was another way the captain showed respect. He was telling Jake it was all right. He wasn't behaving like a coward for leaving.

That didn't make the trip back to the reservation any easier.

They quickly got the President back onto Marine One. The helicopter would fly the President back to Baghdad International Airport, and from there, Air Force One would fly the President back to Washington, D.C.

The President remained silent until Air Force One took off from Baghdad three hours later. It wasn't until he and Jake were alone in the President's private cabin that he said in a quiet voice, "I'm sorry, Jake."

Jake couldn't bring himself to reply.

CHAPTER SEVEN

"This is bullshit," Jess said.

"I know," Jake replied.

"We need to find the traitor."

"Don't say anything about that," he said, "not one word."

On the way home from Iraq, Jess had contacted Jake to inform him that she had detected a series of communications sent to the vicinity of the ambush. There was a message sent when Air Force One landed in Baghdad, a message sent when Marine One landed in Tikrit, and a third message sent when the convoy was fifteen minutes away from the location of the ambush. Jess hadn't been able to verify the origin of the messages, but the channel used was a Secret Service channel, an old one that had been retired ten years ago, but a Secret Service channel, nonetheless.

It could be that Bard had sent the messages using a channel he remembered from his days in the Secret Service, but there was no way that Bard could know the President's movements without an informant. Jess had been able to confirm that the messages came from outside of Iraq, so it wasn't possible for anyone aboard Air Force One or in any of the military bases they visited to have sent the message.

There was a traitor, but while Jake, Jess and Art had been aware of this for months, they couldn't risk showing their hand, especially not now.

"Seriously?" she asked. "Let me just make sure I understand. We're going to sit our butts down and not give the actual reason for the screw up?"

"There was no screw-up," Jake said. "And if we point out the likelihood of an inside job, we might be giving the traitor advanced warning."

She sighed heavily. "This whole situation is bullshit. Here's an impossible-to-control environment. The President should never be there. You don't have the authority to manage the situation to your liking. Just protect the President regardless of all the ways you tell us you can't. A few days later, it's how the hell did you screw this up? How did everything go sideways? What the hell is wrong with all of you?"

"You know it," he said, "and I know it. They know it, too. Make no mistake about that. This is all CYA."

"But whose asses are they covering?"

"Maybe themselves. Maybe someone who suggested to the President it was a good idea. Who knows? We go in there and we take our lumps and get back to work."

"What if they want to give us more than a few lumps?"

"They can't," Jake said. "They can threaten us, but that's it. They'll want us to leave the meeting believing our careers are in jeopardy, but if they take actual action, there will be a real investigation. We'll be called to testify in Congressional hearings. They know we're not to blame. This is all just to make a checkmark on the list of things to do."

"I wish I had your confidence."

"Have a little fun in there," he said drily. "Whatever they ask first, say something about how that was the same question the guy from the Post asked. If they ask your response, tell them you said no comment."

"Are you sure?"

"They're going to ask about dead servicemen and women," Jake said, "and we didn't have any authority over them. They're not calling in actual commanders. This is all for show so they can tell Congresswoman Soundbite or Senator Self-Important that they conducted a thorough and careful review and reprimanded the relevant employees. If this were real, then the one-star who managed the military's side of things would be in front of the chiefs of staff enjoying the most high-profile court martial in American History. It's not real. It's CYA."

"If you say so."

The two of them entered the conference room where the interview would take place. Since this was ostensibly an Internal Affairs investigation, two IA officers were present. Jake wasn't surprised at all to see the IA officers were his old friends Patel and Rodney. The two of them had investigated Jake when past events from his military career had surfaced and called into question his honesty when he applied. Ironically, they could have fired him for not sharing that information. For what happened in Iraq, they could only bluster.

He also wasn't surprised to see that they knew that. They shared an exasperated look with each other as Jake and Jess sat in front of the board.

Aside from Patel and Rodney, Art was there as Jake's and Jess's immediate superior. George Yarborough, the Deputy Director of

Internal Affairs, a sour-faced man of maybe sixty with a pot belly and a physique that made it clear he was a political appointment and had less actual experience with the Secret Service than Jake did with the Boston Celtics, rounded out the review board. The lack of an advocate for Jake and Jess further proved that this whole interview was just posturing.

Yarborough started the questioning. "Will you please state your names for the record?"

Jake resisted the urge to say *Puddin Tane, aske me again, I'll tell you the same.* He gave his actual name, and after Jess gave hers, Yarborough asked, "Can you please describe the sequence of events that led to the loss of fourteen American servicemen on the afternoon of October 23rd?"

"No."

Yarborough flinched as though slapped. Art sighed, and Jake felt a brief moment of sympathy. He and Jess would walk out of here with no repercussions. Art would too, but he would have to attend meetings with Yarborough and no doubt deal with a lot of irritation from the self-important IA director.

"Excuse me?" Yarborough asked.

"You have access to every second of the time from the President's arrival in Iraq to our arrival home. You have camera feeds, audio feeds, itineraries, and a whole host of other sources. This interview is already a waste of time. I don't feel like wasting a second longer than I have to."

Yarborough drew himself up self-importantly. "I assure you, Special Agent, this interview is very serious."

"Very well. We'll cooperate when we're officially charged with a crime."

"Excuse me?"

"Special Agent Foster and I will cooperate with an official investigation should we be charged with dereliction of duty or whatever trumped-up bullshit you decide to throw at us. Until that time, I don't feel like cooperating with your attempt to look pretty in front of Congressional watchdogs."

Yarborough stared at Jake in shock. He looked at the two IA agents, who kept their faces stony but clearly enjoyed seeing their boss embarrassed. He looked at Art, but Art didn't even bother hiding his smile. He reddened and turned to Jess. In his best impression of an angry bear—an impression that came out more like a slightly annoyed weasel—he said, "Does he speak for you, Special Agent Foster."

Jess sighed. “No. I do.”

The corners of Yarborough’s lips curled up into a smile. “Very well. Will *you* please explain to me the series of events that occurred from the arrival of Air Force One in Iraq up until the loss of fourteen American service members?”

“No.”

Art turned around and coughed to hide his laughter. Yarborough huffed and sputtered a few seconds, then said, “Special Agent! This is—”

“Bullshit,” Jess replied, “and I have better things to do.”

Yarborough turned a shade of purple that would have made any eggplant jealous. He looked around at everyone else in the room and shouted, “This is outrageous!”

Finally, Art couldn't hide it anymore. He said, "You're right, George. And so are Special Agents Foster and Mercer. This entire interview is an outrageous, bullshit waste of time. So here's my suggestion: write down whatever you need to in your report to convince yourself that the people who you incorrectly think are coming for your head will be satisfied that you did your due diligence. Do it in your own office, though, away from my agents. As Special Agent Foster so succinctly put it, they have better things to do."

Yarborough’s last flush just barely edged out the plum for the title of most purple fruit. His lip trembled like a child’s. Then he stood and glared at his two agents, who no doubt would get an undeserved earful for their refusal to participate in the charade.

The three of them left, and Art shook his head and looked back at the two of them. “On a serious note, something very wrong did happen out there. Do you two have an idea what?”

“I have an idea,” Jess replied, “but I would prefer to investigate further before I share it.”

“That’s fine,” Art said. “Do what you need to do, and I’ll make sure George doesn’t make things hard for you just to be a pissant. I want to know once you have a conclusion, though.”

“Yes, sir.”

“Wonderful. Dismissed.”

Once they were outside of the interview room, Jess released a sigh. “If you hadn’t talked to me about this ahead of time, I would be dusting off my resume.”

Jake nodded. "It'll be a good idea to pretend. I mean, we should act like there are dire consequences looming over us. We should… that sword. Hang on." He closed his eyes. He couldn't remember. He sighed and said, "That sword hanging over the guy's head."

"Damocles?"

"Yes," he said, "we should act like that Ancient Greek legend."

She laughed lightly. "It's not a legend."

"It really happened? Seriously?"

"No. It's not Greek, either. Cicero wrote it to illustrate how people in power always feared for their lives. Damocles made a comment to king about living a perfect life and…"

"Okay," Jake said, "I don't care. Does it fit the situation?"

She laughed again. "Good enough. So are we done with Yarborough, or do we think he's still going to come for us?"

"Oh, he'll come for us. He's pissed that we made him look like the weakling he really is. He'll definitely leap at the first opportunity."

"So we don't give him an opportunity."

"Exactly."

"Remind me again why we need to go through this stupid charade."

He shrugged. "Because we live in Washington, DC."

She nodded. "We still need to protect ourselves some, right? We can't just completely ignore people who believe their purpose is to keep you and me in line."

"And everyone like you and me. Right. The whole town runs on soundbites, and that happens even when the cameras aren't rolling."

"All right," she said, "then talk to me, genius. What do we do about that?"

"We figure this out. We figure out everything there is to know about Hadad's organization. We find the traitor. We end this whole thing."

She looked at him for a moment and then said, "So we just do what we were doing before?"

"But faster," he replied.

She sighed. "All right. But dinner's on you."

"How does that follow?"

"It doesn't, but dinner's still on you."

As Jake headed to pick up dinner, he wondered how Max could have missed the mark so completely. It was true that Max wasn't trained as an intelligence operative, but he had been so confident before. What had changed? Had Bard misdirected him somehow? If so, was Max in danger?

He sent a message to Max to lay low, just in case. Max agreed to stay away from the Secret Service but told Jake in no uncertain terms that if Trident tried to attack his bar, then Bard would be the one carried out in a body bag.

A part of Jake hoped Bard would try it. He had no doubt Max would keep his promise.

When he returned to Jess's office with hoagies and coffee, Jess had an answer waiting for him.

"Well, that explains a lot," Jake said.

"And here I thought he was just a garden variety asshole," Jess said.

"You'd be surprised how much damage the common asshole can do."

The asshole in question wasn't Niedermayer or Stockton, the two individuals initially suspected to be the traitors. It also wasn't Deputy Director Yarborough, a fact that mildly surprised and—he had to admit—somewhat disappointed Jake.

The asshole in question was the head of the Secret Service's Rapid Response Cadre, a former Army Ranger named Commander Henry Dalton. He wasn't exactly an obvious choice, but as the leader of the most tactically well-equipped division of the Secret Service, he had access to technologies that would—and had—made tracking his actions difficult.

But they had him now. At least, they almost did.

"So what do we do?" Jess asked. "Do we go after him?"

"Not yet," Jake replied. "He has very powerful friends in Congress. We need to get enough evidence to nail him to a wall he can't squirm out from under."

"I'm not sure if your analogy works," Jess said, "but I'll get to work on finding that evidence."

CHAPTER EIGHT

Jake knew Commander Dalton as a reasonably incompetent example of the Peter Principle. Every employee tends to rise to his level of incompetence and in time, every position is occupied by an employee who is incompetent to carry out the post's duties. Dalton had been an excellent Ranger, but the only reason he hadn't utterly botched his Secret Service career was that his field commanders—the captains of the individual Rapid Response Teams—were some of the most excellent tacticians Jake had ever seen.

Jake didn't agree completely with the theory. The fact that the RRT leaders were so exemplary proved that it wasn't an entirely accurate way to look at things.

The first part fit, though, at least in Dalton's case. Dalton had been an excellent ranger, then a competent agent, but he was not a competent commander. He was, in fact, an entirely ineffective commander. He would spend the last third of his career in the same position, never better. Jake couldn't be sure that realizing that is what prompted him to seek accomplishment by betraying his country, but considering Bard's track record of turning disgruntled servicepeople, it fit.

"How are you doing over there," Jess asked.

"Have to check and cross-check everything," he said. "You know, dot every *i*. Cross every *t*."

"Well, you can keep doing that if you like," she said, "or you can come over here and see hard evidence."

"Hard evidence?" he asked, rising from his seat. He walked to where she sat and leaned over to look at her screen. "What am I looking at?"

"This is his personal email account," she said, "and this is the email he got telling him that his personal email is the recovery email for another email account."

"What does that mean?" Jake asked.

"It means there's a secret email account he's trying to keep anonymous, but he's not good at it because he made his personal account the recovery email."

"Okay, I got half of that."

"If you want to do a secret mailbox to receive sexy photos from your Latin mistress," she said, "you pay cash. That way, there's no credit card bill. You don't let the mailbox place have your actual address. If it's secret, you don't want a bill coming to your house. Your wife would find it and go investigate. The next thing you know, she's got an eyeful of Hispanic beauty, and you've got a divorce."

"I'm not married," he replied.

"You don't have a Latin mistress either. You get the point, though, right?"

"I think so. What you found is proof of an email address that's unregistered with the Secret Service. That's suspicious, but it's not evidence of treason."

She smiled and said, "No wonder you don't have a wife. I mean, you constantly underestimate me. You treat me like some twelve-year-old kid who spends all day making game mods and not like a professional. I can only imagine what you'd do to someone you actually kiss. So tell me, big man, does Shiela occasionally tell you no more kisses until you treat her like an adult?"

"What the hell are you talking about?" he asked.

She laughed and tapped the keyboard. "Keep it together. I won't actually ask her about it." The screen disappeared, replaced with a new one.

"What's this?" he asked.

"This? This is the email address, the one that's unregistered with the Secret Service. And this email is evidence of treason. So, in short, this is more than a suspicious situation. I have your traitor for you, and it's settled. So far, there are half a dozen emails that are evidence of treason."

Jake nodded and walked away.

"Where are you going? Aren't you going to say something about never doubting me again?"

"I'm going to talk to this asshole," Jake replied.

"Hang on," she said and stood. The humor was gone from her eyes. "Take a breath, Jake. This man has an uninspired record. He's been passed over and knows he's got nothing better in his future. What he has, though, is an over-inflated sense of worth. He believes should have been promoted, that he's better than people give him credit for."

"All right…" Jake said, "and?"

"That makes him self-righteous. Self-righteousness makes him dangerous. He won't think of this as you catching him. He's going to think of this as you standing between him and what he deserves. He won't hesitate when it comes to trying to kill you."

Jake smiled, unholstered his weapon, and ensured a round was chambered. "I'm counting on that, Jess," he said.

"Damn," she replied, "Ignore everything I just said, then. Instead, just remember that he's more valuable to us alive than dead."

"I'll remember it," Jake said, "For his sake, I hope he does too."

He turned to leave, and she grabbed his shoulder and said, "You're also more valuable to us alive than dead. You're not fully healed, Jake."

At her words, Jake's body decided to remind him of the same fact by sending a twinge of pain through his abdomen. He frowned and pulled away from her. "I'll be fine."

"Jake…"

"I'll be fine. For Christ's sake, I'm not looking to fight him."

"My point is that *he* might fight—"

"I get it, Jess," Jake snapped. He sighed and said more softly. "I'll be careful."

"You've said that before."

"And I'm still alive, aren't I?"

"For now."

He didn't have a response to that, so he just left.

Dalton was in the RRT training compound, a twelve-thousand square foot basement level underneath headquarters. In practice, the RRTs preferred to train with military or FBI units, and the training compound was used as little more than a glorified gym/shooting range.

But Dalton could usually be found there, lifting weights, using the range or completing the obstacle course, no doubt trying to reinforce his belief that he was being sorely underutilized by showing himself how much of a badass he was.

He would learn better today.

Jake found him at the range, which was wonderful because it meant Jake had an excuse to draw his own weapon. Dalton looked at him, then did a double-take. Jake noticed the way his skin paled and stifled a smile. "Hey there, Hank. Mind if I join you?"

After years with the Secret Service and years with the Marines beforehand, Jake was rarely caught off guard. So when the voice that answered him wasn't Dalton's, he actually flinched.

"I would love for you to join us."

Jake whirled toward the voice, and when he saw the owner, his eyes first widened, then narrowed.

The man who smiled back at him from the other end of the range was older than Jake remembered him. His red hair had grayed considerably and was now a roughly even mix of steel and fire. He was still in great shape, but the edges of his muscles had softened somewhat, and his waist appeared an inch or two wider than it had when he had been forced out of the Service.

Still, Eli Bard radiated a strength and command in his aura that made it easy for Jake to understand why so many had fallen under his sway.

"We've been long overdue for a chat anyway."

Jake didn't bother reaching for his weapon. He could see out of the corner of his eye that Dalton had him covered, and even if he could have disarmed the former soldier before Dalton could shoot him, Bared would know doubt draw his own weapon and put an end to their encounter before it got started.

So, he did the next best thing. He reached up to scratch his head, and in the process, tapped his earpiece. He kept his hand up there and rubbed his temples, allowing his anger to bleed through a little to lend legitimacy to the physical actions. "Well, if it isn't the traitor."

"That word's been thrown around so many times it doesn't mean anything anymore," Bard said. "Technically speaking, the entire nation of America was founded by traitors. Had we lost that war, George Washington, Thomas Jefferson, John Adams and all of the other heroes of the revolution would be thought of with the same revulsion as Maximilien Robespierre."

"I could list a dozen reasons why you're wrong about that," Jake said, "Instead, I'm just going to tell you that you're under arrest."

Dalton began to laugh, but a glance from Bard quieted him. "Come on, Jake," Bard began.

"Special Agent Mercer," Jake corrected.

Bard smiled. "Jake. We know that you can't do that. You're a dangerous man, but so am I, and so is Dalton. Besides, you're not close to a hundred percent yet. At your best, you might be able to escape. As you are now, you'd get one of us possibly before the other killed you, but realistically, you'll just end up hurt again. I don't want that."

"Fuck you."

Bard sighed, then spoke with the patient exasperation of a parent speaking to an unruly toddler. "Jake, we can squabble pointlessly, or we can talk. I'd much rather talk."

"So talk," Jake replied. "I'm not stopping you." *Not until backup arrives, anyway.*

Bard shrugged. "Very well. I'd like you to come work with me."

Jake couldn't have stifled the laugh that followed even if he wanted to. "I think you'll find me a lot harder to turn than my friend was."

"Drew isn't nearly as gullible as you think he is. Like you, he threatened to kill me when I first talked to him. Like you, he agreed to hear me out. I hope to convince you to see things from my side, as I convinced him and Commander Dalton behind you."

"So convince me."

"Jake, the system is broken. You know it is. You see every day how the political machinery of Washington exists only to ensure that those in power remain in power and those oppressed remain oppressed. Even your friend, Bryan—"

"That's Mr. President to you."

"No," Bard said calmly. "He is not my president. As Thomas Jefferson said, it has become necessary to break the bonds that now chain us. Your friend, *Bryan*, is the latest warden of those bonds. I'm trying to break them. Look around you, Jake. So many suffer needlessly because everyone here is more concerned about keeping power and not concerned about using it to do good in the world. We're doing good, Jake. Trident is. We're creating a world where one's success depends solely on one's ability and not on one's ability to manipulate and deceive others. Help us build that world."

"They're right outside, Jake," Jess whispered through the earpiece. "Should I send them in?"

"Sure," Jake said, both to Jess and to Bard. "Keep telling yourself that."

He spun around and launched himself at Dalton. At the same time, the door to the compound burst open, and a security team rushed in, weapons drawn.

Jake tried to drag Dalton to the ground, but the traitor knew of Jake's injury and jabbed his fingertips under Jake's ribs. Jake cried out as a shock ran through his body, and his hold on Dalton weakened. Dalton spun, throwing Jake over his hip. Jake landed heavily, and as he got to his feet, another wave of pain forced him to his knees. He was forced to watch as Dalton ran from the room unmolested.

But the reason he was left alone more than made up for his escape.

"Sir," the security team leader said to Jake. "We have the suspect in custody."

Jake managed to make his feet this time, just in time to see Bard glaring at him. He smiled down at the discomfited Trident leader and said, “All right, Bard. Time to have a *real* conversation.”

CHAPTER NINE

Jake couldn't really wrap his head around Bard's sullen defeat. He would have expected defiance and not resigned compliance. Had the man really believed Jake would join him? Jake knew there were people, megalomaniacal people, who couldn't comprehend disagreement. Had Bard really judged him to be the kind of man who would agree to join him?

No.

Bard probably intended the whole thing as a charade. He intended and expected Jake to refuse. It was probably some sort of show for Dalton, some object lesson that Bard wanted Dalton to learn. Bard wasn't defeated because Jake didn't join him. He was defeated because Jake captured him and ruined his plans. Instead of solidifying his authority with Dalton, the situation undermined it.

But it still didn't seem right. Bard was acting defeated now, but Jake couldn't help but wonder if that too was part of some wider plan.

"You know Homeland will be here soon," Jess said.

Bard didn't respond. His eyes, though, showed he didn't need to be convinced. Jake said, "You're going to end up in a hole somewhere. You'll be there forever. After a few months, it won't matter because you'll lose all sense of time. All you'll know is whatever seven or eight square feet of space you have is the only space you'll ever have. All you'll know is that you'll never see sunlight again."

Again, Bard didn't respond.

Jess said, "The only hope you have of anything other than isolation for the rest of your life is to cooperate."

Jake waited until he was sure Bard's eyes revealed complete surrender to that fact. He still didn't trust that surrender as far as Jess could throw Bard, but he didn't have anything else to work with right now.

So, he said, "Tell me about Hadad. What are his plans?"

Bard didn't speak. Jess rolled her eyes and said, "We'll just give him to homeland. Screw this."

She walked toward the door. Jake shrugged and followed her. She reached for the door but didn't get her hand on the knob before Bard said, "Wait!"

Jake turned around and tried his best to appear disinterested. Jess said, "No games, Bard."

"The Western Wall," Bard whispered.

"That's his next target?" Jess asked.

Bard nodded. With his shoulders slumped and his eyes downcast, he looked very bit the fifty-four years of age his file indicated.

Outside the room, Jake imagined Art was busily contacting the White House to inform them of the news. The President's next stop in the Middle East was Jerusalem as part of peace talks to bring an end to the conflict in Gaza. Clearly, plans would have to change based on this revelation.

"When?" Jake asked.

"That's all I know," Bard replied, "he's not…" He looked down at his hands in the cuffs. "He's a colleague," Bard continued, "not a subordinate. I… well, after recent events, I've needed to outsource operations to third parties."

Jake imagined admitting that the Secret Service's successes in Washington D.C. and Paris had crippled his organization was painful for Bard. He turned around, opened the door, and stepped out, signaling with his eyes for Jess to follow him.

Once the door was closed, she said, "He's not the boogeyman I expected him to be."

"He's not *acting* like the boogeyman we expected," Jake replied.

Jess frowned. "You think the whole defeated thing is an act?"

"I'm certain of it," Jake replied, "but that doesn't mean he's lying. We saw with St. Clair that Bard takes it very poorly when his 'colleagues' choose to act against his carefully laid plans. He might still be telling the truth about the Western Wall."

"How do we tell?"

Jake sighed. "I'm not sure. And since the President is scheduled to visit the Western Wall, we need to assume Bard is telling the truth."

"You can't convince the President to stay this time?"

"The President of Israel requested him personally. He's convinced that we have a chance to bring lasting peace to the Middle East."

"And our President believes him?"

"Our President believes that Israel is an important ally in the region and that without Israel to keep the extremists in check, we could look at more terrorist violence."

She sighed. "Right. So what do we do?"

"Well, we know when the attack on the Western Wall will happen."

"How do we know?" she asked. Jake just stared at her again, and she shook her head. "Yeah, okay. I'm an idiot. The attack will happen when POTUS is there."

Jake nodded. "And there's no way we'll get him to cancel the appearance."

Jess asked, "Why don't you talk to Sheila about it? Maybe she could convince him." Taken aback, Jake just stared at her. The comment was entirely inappropriate and there was hint of bitter aggravation in her voice. She smiled, trying to cover it up, and said, "You know, in between times you're hitting the sack with her."

Before he could respond, she started down the hallway. "I'll get to work and see if we can get a bead on location. See if I can get access to Israeli security footage."

Jake stared after her as she walked away. He felt certain he hadn't misheard her tone. It wasn't exactly vitriolic, but she definitely had negative feelings about Sheila. Clearly, she was more upset by their relationship than she had let on. He could understand that. As his partner, her career was affected by his choices even if he'd done nothing wrong. So far, Jake had managed to keep his relationship with the President's daughter from impacting their jobs, but that didn't mean it wouldn't happen at some point. Already, Jake had nearly found himself in several situations where he would have chosen to prioritize Sheila's safety over his job. He'd managed to find ways out of those situations so far, but that wouldn't always be the case.

He couldn't think about that right now, though. There was a great deal of work to do in order to deal with the new information. He hadn't been facetious when he pointed out there was no way they would be able to get the president to cancel the trip. He would just hear more about how the United States didn't let terrorists decide the agenda.

He walked back into the interrogation room and said, "Okay, Bard. This is what's going to happen now. I'm going to keep talking. The answers you give to my questions will determine whether we hand you over to the CIA and let them test inventive new methods of torture the public will never know about on you or whether we keep you in a good old-fashioned supermax jail cell until you're convicted of treason, mass murder and a whole host of other charges and sentenced to good, old-fashioned death by lethal injection. So here's question one: What, in detail, is Hadad planning?"

Bard sighed. "He didn't share details with me. All I can offer is speculation. My speculation is that he will attack from a distance, probably with drones. He prefers to stay away from the front lines. His experience is selling weapons to other people, not fighting himself. That's why he's been so fucking awful at it so far."

"For sure. That's why you've been so much more successful than him at assassinating the President."

Bard glared at Jake, but Jake kept his face stony. He didn't really care about Bard's ego.

"That's all I know," Bard said, "that and Hadad wants it to be a spectacle."

"A spectacle?"

"Yes. He wants people to see it. He wants to be in the news. He wants to embarrass the United States in the most public and newsworthy way possible. He doesn't just want to assassinate the President, he wants to make the Secret Service, the military and the allied nations supporting you look bad. That's why he and I so frequently disagree."

Jake's eyes narrowed. "You're being remarkably free with this information. I have to admit, I expected at least a little pushback from someone who made such a point of being a badass."

Bard's lip curled upward in contempt. "I guess I'm angrier at Hadad's arrogance than I am at yours."

Jake didn't reply right away. That actually made a lot of sense. Bard could just be using the Secret Service to kill a "colleague" who was no longer playing by Bard's rules. It was quite possible that's what had happened with St. Clair when he made his foolish head-on assault on the President's compound in Vilezy-Villacoublay. He may have allowed himself to be captured and allowed Dalton to be a witness to that capture to justify himself to Trident when he inevitably escaped.

"So tell me about Drew," Jake said, shifting tacks. "What brought him to you? Or you to him?"

Bard chuckled. "Drew came to me because he was a patriot. The same reason everyone came to me."

There was that ego again.

"So patriots assassinate their Presidents and kill civilians in the process? Doesn't sound like a new world order I'd like to be a part of."

“That’s because you’re too narrowminded,” Bard said. “You’ve heard the saying that you can’t make an omelet without breaking a few eggs.”

“Have you heard the saying that people aren’t eggs and nations aren’t omelets?”

“The point is still valid even if you don’t like my metaphor. No change has ever occurred without sacrifice. George Washington broke a time-honored and valued Christmas Day truce to ambush the British and the Hessians and allow his army a chance to escape the grip of the enemy. His actions were considered barbarous, heinous, despicable at the time. Was he an evil man because he did what was necessary to win?”

“So you’re the next George Washington.”

“I’m a man trying to change his country for the better. If there was a way to accomplish my goals without acting violently, I would. Keep in mind, Jake, it was years before I used force. I tried everything imaginable to find another way.”

“Like what?”

“Political lobbying, grassroots cultural change, infiltrating academia: you name it, I tried it. I’m not a violent man, Jake.”

Jake decided the conversation was over. He chuckled and said, "All right, Bard. You keep telling yourself that. Better yet, tell your warden. Maybe you can earn yourself an extra five minutes of sunlight."

He tapped the intercom and said, “The prisoner is ready for transport. Get me someone here to shackle him. I want him unable to blink without someone using a key to unlock something. Then I want him on an armed convoy somewhere I’m not allowed to know about.”

He hated that he felt it still wasn’t enough. Bard had been captured easily, but something about it seemed too easy. The security measures they would use to transport him were more sophisticated and more thorough than would be used for any prisoner in history, but…

But there was nothing more Jake could do. He needed to respond to the threat to the President. He stood and left the room without another word. He could feel Bard’s eyes boring into his back as he left, and that did little to improve his mood.

He met Art behind the two-way mirror. The Deputy Director had a scowl on his face, and his arms were folded across his chest.

“What do you think?” he asked Jake.

“He’s not telling us everything,” Jake replied. “I think that what he’s saying is true, but I think he’s holding a lot of information back.”

“So what should we do?”

Jake sighed. “What can we do? I’m assuming that the President told you that canceling Jerusalem was out of the question.”

“He did, and he wanted me to tell you so you didn’t call him and try again.”

“Then we do our best, as we always do, to keep the President safe.”

“Well, yes, but what about him?” Art hooked a thumb at Bard.

Jake looked through the two-way mirror and wasn’t surprised to see Bard staring back at him. Bard couldn’t actually see the two investigators through the mirror, but he knew they were there.

"Lock him in a lead-lined box and don't let anyone see him. He gets his meals through a slit in the door. Absolutely no one talks to him, and he is allowed no technology of any kind."

“Why a lead-lined box?”

“It’s a comic-book reference. I just mean I want him somewhere no one can reach him.”

“Well, we can do that,” Art said. “You think he’s playing us?”

Jake looked at Bard and said, “I’m absolutely sure of it. But that doesn’t mean his information is invalid. He might be chafing under the fact that Hadad isn’t under his thumb, and this could be his way of removing Hadad from the equation.”

“Or it’s his way of lulling us into a false sense of security.”

“I don’t like this any more than you do,” Jake said, “but it’s what we have.”

Art sighed. "Yeah. You're right. I just wish we could decide what we had one of these times instead of relying on terrorists to spoon-feed information to us."

“From your mouth to God’s ears.”

Art frowned. “What?”

“It’s a saying. Christ, don’t be so literal.”

“Screw you, Jake.”

“You too, sir.”

Jake left the room and headed to Jess’s office. Jess had a map open of Jerusalem on one monitor, with maps of the airport in Tel-Aviv, the Western Wall, the Temple of Solomon, and various other landmarks the President’s itinerary would take him to or near.

She smiled at Jake, and any tension he thought she had shown earlier was gone. “Did we put Jack back in the box?”

“For now. Here’s hoping he doesn’t find a way to pop out of it again.”

CHAPTER TEN

Security preparations were difficult, and not just for Jake. An organization like the Secret Service required trust. It was similar to the trust a Marine had to feel for members of his unit. The only difference was that while Marines trusted their brothers to have their backs, Secret Service agents had to trust their comrades to have their backs and the President's back.

Now, that trust was shaken. Jake didn't find it odd that nobody seemed particularly surprised that Dalton was the traitor. The issue wasn't the identity of the traitor, but that there was a traitor in the first place.

At the moment, he and Jess were meeting with representatives from the Israeli Police, the Israeli Defense Forces, and Mossad, the organizations nominally responsible for security at the peace talks. Jake felt a measure of confidence on one level. He didn't know there was any country on Earth more prepared for security than Israel. On the other hand, there were still personalities at play. The police, the Israeli Defense Forces, Mossad, and others all wanted preeminence. Some things, Jake supposed, were universal.

The current haggling was over who should be responsible for the response to any attack. The IDF argued—probably accurately—that they had greater resources and should be the ones allowed to take the lead. Mossad argued that as the nation's premier antiterrorism organization, they had the training and skillset necessary to bring the perpetrators to justice. The Israeli Police reminded both agencies that the top priority was to ensure the attack was unsuccessful and that they had the expertise necessary to ensure that was the case.

Jake pointed out that he couldn't give a camel's ass who took the credit. He just wanted the President of the United States to be safe and would appreciate if everyone else had the same priority. Oddly enough, his point wasn't entirely well-received.

He was grateful when one of the men suggested a five-minute break. A nagging suspicion had risen in his mind during the meeting, and he needed to address it with his partner. He led Jess a short distance away and asked, "What if he was the boogeyman?"

“What?”

"Bard. What if we're wrong? What if he was the boogeyman all along?"

She stared at him for a moment and finally asked, “You think he played us?”

"I know he played us. What I mean is, what if he's *just* playing us?”

“So, no attack here?”

“Actually, I think Bard is the kind of man who might want to show us he can do whatever he wants even if we know about it ahead of time. I also think he might consider it in his best interests to make us think he’s pissed at Hadad when Hadad really is doing exactly what Bard wants him to.”

She didn’t respond right away. Finally, she said, “You might be right about that. He’s definitely got a god complex. What if he got himself detained intentionally?”

"I hate to say it, but I'm beginning to think that's the most logical conclusion."

Again, there was silence. Finally, Jess asked, “So what do we do?”

Jake said, “I don’t think we do anything differently. He may have tricked us into thinking he feels defeated, but we’re still going to defend the president. Best-case scenario, he was lying and Hadad isn’t planning to attack. It’s been a long damned time since I’ve seen a best-case scenario.

Jess chuckled. “You and me both. Same plan?”

“Yes,” Jake said. He glanced around the area. “I’ll set up sniper positions. The Israelis will handle random security checks.”

“And you’ll finalize the escape route?”

“Along with an alternative or twelve,” he said. “You work on the electronic countermeasures.”

“You’re always so romantic,” Jess said with a smile. “Electronic countermeasures? You know how to show a girl a good time.”

Before Jake could figure out the humor in that statement, she looked around and said, “Your contacts are getting antsy. Let’s get to it.”

She turned and walked away, and Jake smiled at her back. She was back to being Jess again. Whatever had happened back in D.C., she was no longer upset with him.

Well, it was probably anxiety that had led to that tension in the first place. The past six months and counting had been filled with constant credible threats against the president. It had him on edge as well. The job was stressful in the best of circumstances. These were most definitely not the best of circumstances.

He headed back to the Israelis. As he walked, he scanned for potential sniper positions. He wanted Secret Service snipers in those positions, but he was under no illusion that the politically minded people he had just spent the past two hours haggling with would allow him that victory.

He was pleasantly surprised when he was able to get through the sniper set up and the evacuation procedures without any conflict. The security checkpoints took a little longer because each agency wanted to participate, but Jake dealt with that by just setting up more checkpoints.

A few hours later, the preparations were determined and either in process or done. Jake returned to his team to review possible attack scenarios they would need to prepare for. They needed to anticipate drone attacks and prepare appropriate countermeasures.

The one part of Bard's interrogation that Jake didn't find suspicious was his assertion that Hadad wanted to be far away from any fighting. It was true that he had attacked the military bunker personally, but that was a one-off compared to every other event Hadad had been involved in. In the Syria attack, he had relied on drones, and in Iraq, he had simply paid people who were already disgruntled with the continued U.S. presence. And Mahmoud had told Jake that Hadad's greatest concern was getting caught. The best way to avoid getting caught was to not be where people were fishing.

The part about wanting a spectacle was easy enough to believe, too, not because Jake necessarily believed that's what Hadad wanted but because he had no doubt it's what Bard would want. Trident's theatrics had been destructive, but they had also been Bard's Achilles' heel. At times when a stealthy, low-profile assault would have been more likely to succeed, Bard had chosen a grand show. It was possible that Bard was bluffing, but Jake doubted it. He thought himself a revolutionary. Like most revolutionaries, he was far more concerned with his image than with his philosophy. If Trident was going to try anything today, they were going to try something big and visible.

Jake's last visit was to the President. Bryan was in a conference room at the hotel, making last-minute adjustments to his speech. He frowned when Jake walked in, but he didn't tell him to leave.

"Mr. President," Jake began without preamble. "This is the deal. You go to the Wall, you give your speech, and you leave. Directly to Marine One." The President's helicopter was parked near the wall, ready to scramble at a moment's notice to evacuate the President. "We go straight home, we don't pass go, we don't collect two hundred fucking dollars. With all due respect, sir, you shouldn't be here, and I'm not interested in explaining to anyone why more American lives are lost today."

"You know," Bryan replied, "you're probably the only man who will say with all due respect, then proceed to imply the most disrespectful accusation you could possibly make. Since you're my friend, or at least you were my friend, I won't have you removed from your position and barred from future government service, but I also won't hear you accuse me of causing the deaths of any serviceman. For the final time, Jake, we *do not* allow terrorists to dictate our actions. Far more Americans die that way than by making it clear that nothing will cause us to bend. At the very least extend me the courtesy of believing that I believe that, and that I am acting the way I am to minimize American deaths.

"You're a Secret Service Agent, Jake. Your job is simple. It might not be easy to accomplish, but it's easy to understand. My job isn't, so do me a favor and stop moralizing from the pencil-thin worldview your job description allows you to have."

Jake didn't respond right away. It would be a lie to say that Bryan's words didn't sting, but it would also be a lie to say the President didn't have a point. Jake hated politics and all of the dishonesty and manipulation and machinations that came with it, but politics and all of its trappings existed, and the President didn't have the luxury of pretending they didn't the way Jake did.

Still, Jake needed it to be clear what the plan for the President's movements would be. "That being said, sir, I *am* in control of your itinerary today."

"For now."

Jake didn't bother arguing further.

***

The ceremony began without incident. The first speaker was the Israeli president, a dignified, bespectacled man who spoke gravely about solidarity and unity and human rights and all the other buzzwords that showed up whenever anyone discussed the Middle East.

While President Yakob spoke, Jake checked in with Jess. "How are we doing?"

"So far so good. Nothing out of the ordinary. No ghost communications, no EM spikes, no weird signals, and no sign of drone activity. We might get out of this one, okay."

“Let’s not count our chickens before they pull AKs out of nowhere,” Jake replied, “but I’m glad to hear things are going smoothly so far.”

“Where the hell do you get your metaphors?” Jess asked. “God, my ears are bleeding.”

“Bold of you to assume your humor is any better,” Jake fired back.

“It’s not an assumption any more than it would be to assume Wayne Gretzky is a better hockey player than you.”

“I don’t know. He’s been retired for a long time. I think I might have a shot against him now.”

“I’ll be sure to call him when we get back home. I would love to watch you get embarrassed.”

“It’s a date.”

“Don’t say that.”

“What? It’s a date?”

“Yes. Don’t say that.”

“Why?”

“Just… forget about it.”

He smiled. “Aww, is Jess upset that she lost a verbal sparring match for once?”

There was a half-second pause before Jess said, “Sure. That’s what it is.”

Jake turned his attention back to the venue. From his vantage point, he could see the entire section of the wall that was cordoned off for the event. There was nothing that struck him as out of the ordinary so far, but he knew it would only take an instant for that to change in the worst way possible.

Still, when the President began his speech and made it fifteen minutes into his oration with no sign of interruption from terrorists, he began to hope that they might actually get out of this one okay as Jess had said.

Hope springs eternal, but it was just as often dashed as realized. Jake was disappointed and angered but not surprised to hear shouting from outside of the venue, followed by a terse message from his ground forces leader that they were under attack from an unknown number of armed militants.

He tapped his earpiece. “Jess, what are we looking at?”

“We’re looking at proof Bard’s a liar,” Jess said, her voice taut with anger. “No drones, no hidden infiltrators, no EM jamming. Just a damned big force of people with machine guns, rocket launchers, assault rifles and vehicles heading toward the Wall.”

“When you say damned big, how big are we talking?”

“Well, let me put it this way. I hope IDF won at least a few of the contests you were refereeing a few hours ago, because we’re going to need military type resources.”

Jake felt his heart sink. He heard an explosion in the distance and looked beyond the wall to see well over two hundred terrorists swarming toward the wall.

Bard hadn’t lied to them entirely. The attack was taking place exactly where and when he said it would. It was a spectacle. It was grandiose overkill.

And as Jake had suspected, it was proof that Bard could act however he wanted whether he was in custody or not.

CHAPTER ELEVEN

The gathered crowd quickly became aware that the sounds they were hearing weren't cheering and fireworks. There was a moment of shocked stillness followed immediately by panicked running. Jake had assigned crowd control to the Israeli Police Force and was gratified to see that they were at least handling that job relatively well. The purpose of crowd control was twofold: first, obviously, was to evacuate the civilians safely, but second was to ensure they didn't get in the way of the VIPs.

Mossad was responsible for their own President's safety, and Jake wasn't surprised to see a swarm of men and women in plainclothes surround Yakob and immediately spirit him away.

That left Jake's job. He quickly dialed Special Agent Dawson. Special Agent Harkness was still recuperating from the injury to his arm suffered in the Syria attack, an injury that would probably force him out of the President's personal security detail. Special Agent Dawson was the new head of the detail, and while he was a brave and capable agent, he had only a few years of experience, and it showed in the tension in his voice when he answered Jake.

"What should we do, sir?"

Jake put what he hoped was a calming amount of confidence and authority in his voice. "You get LION out of here. That's your only job and your only goal. You get him through one of the escape routes. I don't care which one but tell me when you decide. You get Lion secured. That's it. We clear?"

"Yes, Sir," he said.

"Wonderful. Once Lion is secured, contact me. If I don't answer, Marine One leaves without me. Understood?"

"Yes, sir."

"Outstanding. You got this, Dawson. Let's show these assholes why we beat them every damned time."

It was a slight breach of protocol for Jake to include that little motivational aside, but the extra confidence in Dawson's voice when he replied, "Yes, sir," made the breach worth it.

His next call was to Air Force One. As usual, the President had insisted that his family be allowed to join him on his trip, but at least this time, he had allowed Jake to keep them on Air Force One.

The phone was picked up by Special Agent Trent, the head of Sheila's personal security team and the de facto head of the First Family's security as the most senior agent aboard Air Force One.

"Trent, we're under attack."

Trent also broke protocol by offering a sarcastic, "What a shock," in reply. He followed it with a perfectly acceptable query. "Should we get airborne?"

"ASAP. Tell the Air Forces—both of them—what's going on. I'll call you when Marine One is airborne so you can land in time to pick LION up."

He didn't need to tell Trent not to wait for him. Trent was a seasoned agent with nearly a decade of experience. He understood that the priority was the President and his family, and anyone else was expendable.

He called Dawson and told Dawson to call Trent the moment Marine One was airborne, just in case something happened to himself. Then he called the Marine contingent attached to the President's entourage.

"All right, Marines," he said, "Let's go kick some terrorist ass."

The Marine commander, a major who unlike many field-grade officers was as hardnosed as his Marines, replied, "We're just waiting on you, Staff Sergeant. You forget how to run when you left the Corps?"

"Left the Corps? I don't know what you mean, sir."

Major Dunaway laughed. "I'll see you in a moment, Marine."

On the way to the defending forces that were now engaged with the terrorists, he saw seven or eight U.S. Marines as well as various Israeli soldiers. He rushed toward them and shouted, "Marines, to me!"

Most of them hesitated, not immediately recognizing Jake, but then one corporal shouted, "Yes, Sir!" and started Jake's direction. Jake thought he looked familiar but didn't ask about that now.

He called to the Israelis, "Come on. The more the merrier."

Jake asked the Israelis, "Are you guys cut off?" That was the best explanation for why they ended up with U.S. forces.

One of them nodded and said in slightly accented English, "Our radio man went down. We got him out of harm's way, but we have no communication with our commanding officer."

Jake nodded. "I have to make a call, and then you can use my radio." He had the earpiece, so the radio was really just a backup. "In the meantime, you can help me and my brothers kill a whole lot of asses."

The Israeli smiled. "Well kill the asses with you but stay alive so we can call our superiors once they're dead."

Jake didn't quite follow the man's broken English, but he got the gist of what the Israeli meant. "Deal.'

He quickly radioed Jess. "Jess, I'm switching to the earpiece. This radio's going to a squad of IDF who got separated from their commanding officer."

"Sounds good. Be careful, Jake. Remember, you're not—"

"A hundred percent. I know. I'll do my best, Jess, but at some… well, we'll talk about it later."

"Just make sure you're around to talk about it later."

He signed off and handed the radio to the Israeli. The model was fairly standard, and the Israeli soldier had no trouble changing frequencies and calling his commander to inform them that he and his squad were joining a group of Americans and heading to the fighting.

Jake and the soldiers with him had just made it outside of the wall and were crossing the short distance to friendly lines when he saw something ahead of him in the sky.

"Those look like drones to you?" he asked nobody in particular.

One of the Marines said, "Has to be. Unless pterosaurs made a comeback, and no one told us."

As the drones approached, Jake could see that they were indeed far larger than the ones used in Syria. They were clearly military in origin, too, and that meant they would have at least some form of basic EM hardening. It wouldn't be so simple as jamming them this time.

"Damn it." He tapped his earpiece. "Deploy the countermeasures, Jess. Please tell me you can deploy the countermeasures."

"Hey," she said, "this is me you're talking to. Of course, I can deploy the countermeasures. I can't believe you're even asking. In fact, I'm going to make you pay for asking."

"Make me pay later and deploy the damned things."

"Already in process. I see about a dozen drones. Hang on."

He looked at the men. "Anybody have field glasses?" One of the Israelis handed him a pair of binoculars.

Jake scanned the battle ahead and found that the IDF had quickly assembled a force that matched that of the terrorists. The attackers were holding their position behind cover, but they were unable to advance.

At least not until the drones arrived.

Jake addressed the men with him, “Okay. New plan. I want all but one of you to circle around to the far end of the wall. You see a hostile, you don’t bother communicating or capturing. You take the ass out. Clear?”

“Who stays?” One of the Marines asked.

“You do now. Stay by me. We’ll monitor the drones.”

The others started off. "Are we clear on the directions?" he asked.

“Introduce them to God,” one of the Marines said.

“Outstanding,” Jake replied.

Jake unshouldered his pack and quickly removed his rifle. He was glad he had brought it this time. After being stuck with nothing more than a handgun in Iraq, he wanted to make sure he had the right weapons for the job before he was caught with his pants down again.

“Drones approaching at a speed of about thirty knots,” the Marine who remained behindsaid, looking through the field glasses. “Altitude one hundred meters. Fanning out into a staggered assault pattern.”

Jake lifted his rifle and aimed at the nearest drone. He readied his shot and fired. The drone exploded, which didn’t make a great deal of sense. He quickly said into the radio, “Did you help with that, Jess?”

“No,” came the reply, “I think they’re wired for ramming.”

“Ramming? What do you mean? Like kamikaze stuff?”

“That was an explosion. It wasn’t just the drone breaking apart. That’s my best guess, Jake.”

Lovely. “Anything working on your end?”

“I’m screwing up their navigation,” Jess said. “That’s why they’re changing formation and then reforming and then changing it again.”

The Marine confirmed that a moment later. “They’re all over the place, sir. I can’t tell if they’re trying something randomized and they’re just programmed really poorly or if they’re malfunctioning somehow.”

He looked at the Marine. The name on his helmet was Herzog. Jake went with rank instead. "Sergeant," he said, "we need to take out these drones before they reach friendly forces. They're armed with explosives, and we believe they intend to crash into friendlies.

“Yes, sir,” he said.

“Take aim,” Jake said, “and fire at will.”

He doubted that Herzog would be very effective at this distance, but if he could take out one drone for every two Jake took out, they'd be okay.

Jake aimed and fired. The drone jerked out of the way. They had at least rudimentary evasive abilities. He fired again, this time anticipating the evasion, and the drone exploded.

It took him a moment to realize the drones weren't actually heading closer. They were flying in circles. "Jess, is that you?"

Jess's reply chilled him to the bone. "No. I was wrong. We're not jamming them at all. They're flying exactly as they were programmed to fly. Those jerky movements are just to make us think that we're succeeding. I've analyzed the explosion. It's fulminate of Mercury. It makes a loud bang and a lot of smoke but has very little explosive force.

"Damn it," he spat out. "This is a distraction!"

"What do you mean?" Herzog asked.

"The drones aren't intended to do any damage. It's a diversion." To the radio, he said, "Dawson, are you there?"

"I was just about to call you, sir. Marine One is airborne and proceeding to Tel-Aviv."

Jake looked toward the drones, fearing that with the helicopter in the air, the drones would change course and attempt to shoot the President down. Instead, the drones continued their jerky movements.

What the hell was Hadad doing?"

"Marine One, please be advised of the possibility of aerial and ground threats on your route. The assailants' behavior is unpredictable at the moment."

That was a fancy way of saying that he had no idea what the hell was going on.

"We'll keep our eyes peeled, sir," Dawson replied. "I just confirmed with IDF that they're sending an aerial escort to watch over us."

As if on cue, Jake heard the roaring of turbofan engines and looked up to see two F-35s heading toward Marine One. One of them opened its weapons bays and fired two heat-seeking missiles. The missiles streaked toward the drones, and when they exploded, the tightly packed drones followed. When the smoke cleared, Jake could see a single drone wing fluttering toward the ground.

That took care of that problem.

Herzog cheered, and over his earpiece, Jake could hear Jess doing the same. Her cheering stopped abruptly after a moment, though. "Jess?"

"Shh, hold on."

He waited silently for a moment. Then Jess said, "Jake, we have a lead on Hadad! One of the assailants surrendered and said that Hadad is here in Jerusalem."

Another thing Bard lied about. "Any idea where?"

"There are underground tunnels dating from the first century CE. They were used by early Christians escaping persecution from the Romans. Think the Catacombs but a lot older and more primitive. The captured assailant doesn't know for sure, but he believes that if Hadad were going to hide anywhere, it would be in those tunnels.

"Understood," Jake said. "I'll form a team and lead them underground."

"Sounds good. Unfortunately, that was only the good news."

Jake frowned. "What's the bad news?"

"Guess."

Jake's frown deepened. He nearly scolded Jess about joking around at a time like this.

Then he understood.

"Bard?"

"Yes. He escaped ten minutes ago. No one knows where he is."

"How? How did he escape? For God's sake, he was under more guard than the President!"

"The official story is that the team was ambushed by a terrorist force led by Commander Dalton. The unofficial belief is that there were Trident operatives among the transport convoy."

Jake sighed. "Dammit. How many dead?"

"Nineteen."

"Jesus. And no sign of him?"

"No. He's gone underground."

Jake thought of the tunnels he was about to run through chasing Hadad. He believed a moment ago that at the end of those tunnels, he would find the final threat to the President's safety.

How foolish that belief seemed now.

CHAPTER TWELVE

Jake felt a great deal of trepidation as he led the commandos into the tunnels. Mossad had insisted on being involved in the hunt for Hadad, and knowing both how seriously Mossad took an assault on Israeli territory and how capable Mossad was, Jake had agreed.

The rest of the Secret Service were on their way home. The President had reached Air Force One without incident, and the plane was, by Jake's calculations, just passing the southern tip of Portugal right now. Jake and Jess were the only agents left behind.

He would never have been allowed to lead the hunt for Hadad under ordinary circumstances. Regardless of his experience, he wasn't a Marine anymore. He was Secret Service now, and this fell far outside of his purview. But he had rescued the President once more, and that gave him some leverage. He didn't feel guilty about using that leverage.

Now, though, as he navigated the narrow, man-made caves, he couldn't deny that part of him wished he was literally anywhere else. In the daytime with lighting and a smiling tour guide he might like the place. Now, though, felt a little like a girl in a horror movie. The audience kept yelling, "Don't go in there!" but she always did.

He imagined that part of his trepidation had to do with his experiences in Paris. He had never visited the Catacombs, but he had followed a lead into a sewer running beneath the Paris Metro subway system, and that had ended with him nearly being stabbed to death by a genocidal biochemist. Even though he had a team of commandos with him this time, his skin still crawled.

He had to move carefully now. There was little doubt in his mind that these circumstances were perfect if Hadad wanted to lure them into a trap. There were few places Jake could imagine that would work better for a trap than these tunnels. They were dark, treacherous. They echoed with the sound of running water.

The echoes made maintaining a sense of direction very difficult, but perhaps worse than the echoing water were the occasional silences. They seemed to arrive out of nowhere. It was as though some giant celestial creature turned a faucet off occasionally. The silence seemed as deep as the tunnels seemed dark.

Jake allowed for the possibility that the echoes and silences added to his worry. Nobody with his combat experience could dismiss that. Sometimes, the entire point of psychological warfare was to keep the enemy on edge when nothing threatened them at all. Hadad's constant attacks definitely kept everyone on edge. He had to react to the actual circumstances and not imagined circumstances.

Of course, the ambush hit the moment he came to that conclusion.

Gunfire echoed through the tunnels. The mercenaries attacking, though, operated under the same constraints as Jake and his team, and unless Bard had convinced a team of Delta Force operatives to join him, the attackers weren't nearly as capable as the commandos under his command. Paradoxically, a lot of Jake's worries eased now that the fighting had begun.

He slid to a slight depression in the wall and said into his radio, "We're under attack, Jess." To the commandos, he said, "They can't see us. Lay down suppressive fire at will."

The purpose of suppressive fire was, primarily, psychological. It wasn't intended to actually cause damage. Because Jake and the Israelis were under the same constraints as the attackers, attempting real damage was foolish. The suppressive fire's goal was to make the enemy feel constrained. The entire purpose was to keep the enemy from performing tasks. You had to make them feel like doing anything other than seeking cover would kill them. In some cases, the pressure could cause the enemy to become suicidal, breaking cover and hoping a blitz attack would allow them to escape. Jake wouldn't mind taking a few bad guys out that way, but he wouldn't hold his breath.

The commandos, of course, performed the task well. He saw them moving forward and firing. The muzzle flashes gave away their locations, but it didn't matter. The mercenaries fired only very sporadically. They didn't have the leadership they needed to keep them organized.

That could change at any minute. Jake would put the Secret Service's RRTs up with any tier one operator on Earth, at least in these circumstances, but in France, the arrival of a single sniper had been enough to completely derail the RRTs success.

Jake reached down and found a flare in his fatigues. He took a breath and called into the radio, "I want a kill from each of you. One kill."

He pulled the tab, and the flare ignited. That drew fire immediately, and he heard the bullets hitting the wall close to his head. He threw the flare toward the mercenaries and ducked down just before one of those bullets hit the wall exactly where his skull was a moment ago.

The flare illuminated mercenaries as it flew through the air, and immediately, gunfire sounded from Jake's commandos. Jake saw two mercenaries hit the ground dead before the flare did. The light from the flare wasn't nearly as powerful on the stone walkway as it was in the air, but it illuminated the enemy's position enough that two more mercenaries fell before one was able to reach the flare and kick it into the water.

Jake wondered why he suddenly thought of the attackers as mercenaries. That was what they were, of course. They were soldiers of fortune being paid by Hadad or possibly Trident to fight American and Israeli forces right now, but the term still struck him as strange. They were terrorists, not mercenaries. Maybe he was subconsciously separating the evil of Bard and Hadad from the evil of those who worked for them.

Jake heard the disappointing sizzling sound as the flare hit the water. It would burn for a while, but as it submerged, it gave only the slightest glow that grew dimmer with each passing second. "Suppressive fire," Jake commanded.

While the Mossad agents complied, Jake tapped his earpiece. “Jess, can you give me anything?”

“I can tell you that there are about four dozen mercenaries between you and a large cavern that’s emitting a powerful EM frequency.”

Jake noted that Jess also referred to the terrorists as mercenaries. “What kind of EM frequency?”

“I’m going with a jamming frequency, but it’s just a guess. If it *is* a jamming frequency, it’s not working.”

“Or it’s working so well that it’s disguising its purpose.”

“That too.”

“All right. I need a way there.”

“Pick your poison, and I use the word literally. There’s no trick way in. You’ll just have to fight.”

Jake sighed. “All right. Let’s fight then. Tell me what I need to do.”

“Keep pressing forward. The mercenaries are just trying to hold you. If you push them, they’ll wilt under the pressure.”

“Got it.”

He called out, “Move forward!” then started forward himself, rifle at the ready.

The battle commenced in earnest as Jake and his team started forward. The mercenaries were ill-equipped to handle the crack fighters, but they most definitely didn’t wilt under the pressure. They fought back with an almost religious tenacity.

That meant they weren’t mercenaries. No mercenary force fought with such fanaticism. They were fighting for something they believed in. Jake wasn’t sure what that might be, but from his brief experience with Bard, he wouldn’t have been surprised to find that they fought for him.

How was it that the most persuasive and charismatic people in history were so often evil? Why couldn’t people be persuaded to fight so zealously for the side of good and right?

Jake heard a cry from his left and turned to see one of the Mossad agents had fallen, his arm struck by a rifle round. He cursed and rolled over, using his uninjured hand to continue firing at the terrorists. One of his companions knelt next to him and quickly bound the wound, then helped the injured man to his feet.

Jake smiled grimly. There were zealous people also on the side of good and right, and in the end, Bard would only be one of many megalomaniacs who learned that the hard way.

The question was, would Jake's zeal be enough to keep him going? His physical condition had improved dramatically since the trouble with Hadad began, but as Jess was so fond of reminding him, he was still far from one hundred percent. His wound ached, and his stamina waned slowly but unavoidably. He fought to push the effects away, but each yard cost more and more of his energy.

The team took what cover they could find as they battled the mercenaries. The tunnels were lit only by the flashes of rifle fire. Jake’s team was equipped with night vision goggles, but in the dense black of the tunnel, even those goggles provided only slight visibility.

Jake fired and heard a cry as one of the terrorists dropped. Another fell on top of the one Jake had shot, struck by a Mossad bullet.

Jake felt a strong hand pull him to the ground just before the wall above his head was hit by a terrorist round.

“Stay low,” Zohan hissed.

Jake heeded the warning, as much because he lacked the energy to stand as because he agreed with the advice. He gritted his teeth and aimed his rifle, firing twice. One round went wide, but the second one felled the terrorist who had shot at him.

The terrorists continued to fire on the team, but the superior training of the Mossad commandos showed. One by one, terrorists fell, and one by one, their shots missed their mark. Finally, the rest of the terrorists broke.

Jake's team showed no mercy. These terrorists had killed civilians and planned to kill more. The Israelis had experience with terrorists who killed innocents, and they had learned the hard way that to spare a terrorist one day was to die at his hands the next.

When it was over, Jake tried to stand, but a wave of dizziness came over him as soon as he reached his feet. He collapsed to his knees, shaking and breathing heavily.

One of the Mossad agents leaned down beside him. "Are you all right? Are you hit?"

"I'm fine," Jake said. "Old injury. I'm okay."

The Mossad agent shared a look with one of his fellows that suggested he didn't believe Jake's assertion that he was fine, but he didn't protest. Jake forced himself to his feet and tapped his earpiece. "The enemy is down, Jess. How close are we to the cavern?"

"It should be right in front of you."

Jake frowned at the narrow tunnel ahead and said, "How far?"

"According to your heart monitor and my layout of the tunnels, about thirty feet."

Jake sighed. "Well, it's not here, so—"

"Sir!" one of the Mossad agents called. "Look!"

Jake looked and saw a ladder leading down into a deeper level of the caverns. He frowned. "Jess, can you confirm there are no more hostiles?"

"None that I can pick up on infrared. Why?"

"The cavern isn't right in front of us. It's below us."

"Ah," Jess said. "Well, if there's anything there, I can't see it."

Jake exercised caution anyway as he led the team down the ladder. At any moment, he expected an ambush to pop up out of nowhere and try to attack them, but they reached the bottom of the ladder without further incident.

The cavern was an impressive structure, a forty by fifty-foot room supported by thick stone columns. The smoothness of the walls and the design of the columns suggested this place was a much later addition to the tunnels and not as ancient as the tunnels were up to this point.

Of more interest to Jake, though, was the computer terminal in the center of the room. Jake couldn't crack through the firewall, but the flash drive he attached was able to download the data contained in the computer.

"Jess, I'm sending some data your way. I want you to work on decrypting it. Let me know when you figure out what it is. We're heading back topside."

"Roger. Are we heading home?"

"I don't know yet," Jake replied.

"Fair enough. Be safe."

"Always."

Jake led the team back to the top of the tunnels. Other than the one injured agent, they had accomplished the mission without casualties. Jake took a measure of encouragement in that. The last time he'd been in this situation, he had lost eight Secret Service agents. These men weren't his countrymen, but they were allies, and they had put their lives on the line to help him combat a threat to his nation's president. He was glad he was able to bring them home safely.

He could only hope that he would get so lucky next time.

CHAPTER THIRTEEN

As he and Jess rode through Jerusalem, the crowds and traffic grated on him. “How far away are we?” he asked.

Before the driver could respond, Jess said, “about a mile and a half.”

“Stop the car,” Jake said. The driver looked confused but obeyed. Jake jumped out.

"Hang on!" Jess called. "I'm coming!" He didn't slow down, but soon she was next to him as he walked at a very fast pace.

He felt almost disappointed in Hadad. It was a foolish way to feel, he knew. Still, the idea that he wanted to kill the President as part of a business strategy made no sense. It seemed like something out of a comic book villain’s playbook. Kill the President. Wait for the resulting instability and wars that result. Provide the warring parties with guns.

It was all so damned banal.

When Jess first told him that the files he had recovered from Hadad’s underground facility were plans to profit off of the President’s assassination, he assumed that it was a joke or some sort of pathetic attempt at misdirection again. The more they looked at the plans, the more that he realized it wasn’t a joke but actually the terrorist’s strategy.

God, what an idiot. People like Hadad didn’t do well in times of instability. Their bread and butter was slipping through the cracks of a structure. If the structure collapsed, there would be no cracks, just rubble. When there were cracks, rats like Hadad slipped through them easily. When the cracks were gone, rats fared very poorly against the much larger predators who were no longer held outside the walls.

Speaking of walls, or rather one Wall in particular, what in God’s name possessed Bryan to come back here? For God’s sake, what point did he think he was making?

It occurred to Jake bitterly that it was pointless to keep asking this question, pointless to expect the President to ever think logically about the situation. He was convinced that he had to be Napoleon or Churchill or Lincoln or God knows who and demonstrate the strength of the United States by demonstrating the stubbornness of its president.

Instead of flying home, the President had flown to Germany. Instead of prioritizing his safety, he had prioritized the need to bite his thumb at the terrorists.

So he was coming back to the Wall, this time to give another speech and make a big show about how the free world would no longer hide in fear from terrorists but would fight back and prevail due to morality or some bullshit. Jake didn't understand why the President couldn't make that point from the Oval Office the way every other President had made since the damned White House was constructed.

Well, it wasn't as though Jake's opinion ever mattered. He was just the person who had to clear the way for His Royal Idiocy.

He had to exercise a great deal of self-restraint to keep from pushing people out of the way as he and Jess weaved through dense foot traffic. The ceaseless hum of chatter and the sporadic honk of frustrated drivers irritated him more than it should have. Really, it wasn't the crowd that irritated him, but the situation. He just hated that they had to do this all over again.

And then, there it was. The Western Wall seemed different coming upon it from this direction. It towered above them. The time-weathered stones stacked upon each other formed an imposing sight. There were those who would say the surface of the wall testified to centuries of prayer and tears. To Jake, it spoke of longsuffering patience and survival.

And at the moment, it spoke of the misguided hubris of one man who couldn't accept that the way he felt things ought to be done wasn't working.

"Any changes to the plan we discussed?" Jess asked.

"Nope," he replied curtly. "Get to it. I'll coordinate with the others."

Jess's job was to set up electronic surveillance. He wanted not a single square inch unmonitored.

"On it," she replied.

She headed to the room Mossad had prepared for her and Jake headed to the conference room where he would brief the leaders of the individual teams who would be assisting with the coming event. When he walked into the room, he was somewhat gratified to see that everyone else present seemed as upset about the situation as he was. Maybe that wasn't a helpful attitude to have, but he was at least glad to see he wasn't the only intelligent person left.

"All right," he said, "None of us are happy about being here again, but this is the situation we find ourselves in, so we're going to make do.

This time, we're going to do it without any squabbling. Are we agreed on that?"

The IDF and Israeli Police captains frowned, but all present nodded in agreement. Jake noticed a slight hint of approval on the Mossad leader's face. Jake's success leading the Mossad team through the tunnels had reached his ears, and he viewed Jake with a great deal more respect now.

That was good. Jake would need allies.

"Israeli Police is in charge of perimeter security. No one gets in unless they're Police, IDF, Mossad or Secret Service." The Israeli Police leader raised his hand, and Jake said, "Go ahead."

"A preselected number of press agents have been granted access," the captain informed him. "My officers have their names, ID numbers and photographs. I can forward you the list if you'd like."

"Do that," Jake said. He would send that information to Jess later. "IDF will be responsible for quick reaction forces. Merrick." Commander Gayle Merrick, the acting commander of the Secret Service's Rapid Response forces since Dalton's betrayal was revealed, nodded acknowledgement. "You'll work with Major Chaim. In the event of a terrorist attack, your forces will work together to create an effective response."

"Yes, sir."

"Preston." The Special Agent in charge of the Secret Service's general security contingent nodded. "Your agents are responsible for securing the portion of the wall that will be used to speak and also for securing the escape routes. You will need to coordinate with Mossad, Israeli Police, the RRTs, and the Air Force and Marine Corps to ensure that forces are directed where they need to be when they need to be. The military will be limiting their involvement to threat response and extraction this time so there are no more incidents of muddled command chains."

While the Marines who served with Jake during the last assault on the wall had performed well and were commended for their service, the Marine Corps wasn't especially happy with the disjointed nature of the defense and wanted to be held in reserve so if an attack occurred, there was no confusion about where they needed to go.

"Perfect." Jake tapped his earpiece. "Dawson?"

"I'm here, sir."

Here was on board Air Force One. As head of the President's personal security detail, Dawson would never leave the President's side. He was attending this mission via satellite connection.

"You know what your job is," Jake said simply.

"Yes, sir."

"Wonderful. As before, my partner, Special Agent Foster, will be handling surveillance and electronic countermeasures. She will also be facilitating communications. Does anyone have any questions?"

The looks on everyone's faces told Jake that like him, the question they had was why in Hell they were here to begin with. Like them, Jake had no answer.

Aloud, they voiced their understanding of the plan. Jake finished with, "All right. We have one hour before the event begins. Get into position, and if anything at all looks fishy to you, I want to know about it before the thought forms in your head. Understood?"

They voiced their agreement, and Jake said, "Dismissed."

He headed from the conference room to the surveillance room where Jess was setting up the electronic countermeasures they had prepared. They had brought their own drones this time, CIA models that their contact Mr. Quartz had sent to Israel immediately upon hearing about the first attack on the Western Wall. The drones weren't armed, but they had powerful EM jamming equipment and were themselves hardened against EM attack. They would prove invaluable in the event of another drone assault.

"All right," Jess said, "Looks like we're all good to go. Are you here to talk to the big man?"

"Yes."

"Do you want me to clear the room?"

"Can you for a few minutes and still keep on top of your job?"

"Oh yeah. I have a thousand alarms set to go directly to me if anything's off by so much as a millimeter."

"Great. I can't wait to figure out what crazy thing will happen next to find the one crack we didn't know we had in our plan."

Jess smiled and surprised Jake by kissing him on the cheek. "Relax, Jake. We've come out on top every round. Just because we haven't knocked the opponent out yet doesn't mean we're not ahead on the scorecards."

"True," he said, "but I'd rather not leave this one in the hands of the judges.

"I know what you mean."

She stepped outside, and Jake sat in front of the radio. He tapped a command, and a moment later, the President's face showed up onscreen.

"I know what you're going to say, Jake, and my answer's final. This is necessary to prevent the free world from falling into the trap of fear."

"I understand your position, sir," Jake said. *So save the moralization for your campaign*, he wanted to say but didn't. "And you understand mine."

Bryan returned a tight smile. "One whiff of danger, and I'm back on Air Force One and on my way stateside before I get a chance to know where the smell's coming from."

"Yes, sir."

"I get it. And my family remains on board Air Force One, which will take off the moment I step off and remain airborne until it's time for me to leave."

"Yes, sir. Escorted by Air Force jets."

"I still don't know how you talked Hawkes into giving you carte blanche over military resources. I still have to give him an invoice for the amenities I use on Air Force One."

Jake allowed himself a smile. "Secretary Hawkes takes your security very seriously."

"I guess so. So how are you doing, Jake?"

"I'll execute my duties to the fullest extent of my abilities, sir."

"That's not the question I asked."

"No, sir, but it's the answer you'll get."

Bryan met his eyes for a moment, then decided it wasn't worth pushing his erstwhile friend. He nodded and said, "All right. I guess it's time to get this show on the road."

Jake almost told the President to break a leg, then considered that was probably not the most appropriate response, all things considered. Instead, he said, "Good luck, sir."

"You too, Jake."

He switched off the connection. Jake sat where he was for a long moment, hoping to settle his thoughts and approach the coming storm with some semblance of calm.

He gave up on that after a few minutes. Calm would come after this whole mess was over, and they were back in Washington, D.C. where they belonged.

He sighed and got to his feet. He walked outside and sent Jess back into the room, then headed to his vantage point high up on a building overlooking the wall.

Time to get this show on the road, he thought. *Hope this one's not a shitshow like the last one.*

CHAPTER FOURTEEN

From his roost at the top of the building, Jake looked over the scene. On one level, there was a great deal of comfort and familiarity in taking a sniper's position. To be an effective sniper requires patience. The training in that regard was very clear. He once trained by simply remaining in place for seven hours. That was it. No movement was tolerated by the instructors. That kind of control and patience required a lot of work in the beginning. The USMC Scout Sniper had to be able to maintain a position indefinitely, in some cases waiting twelve hours or longer just for a single shot.

Just being in a sniper position calmed him. The training took over. Without consciously deciding to, Jake regulated his breathing. Without consciously intending to keep his movements slow and measured, he did. Without actively deciding to use relaxation techniques, he did. It allowed him to survey the scene below him with efficiency. He accomplished this efficiently but felt unhurried and unrushed as he surveyed the crowd beneath him gathered at the Western Wall.

He realized it had been a long time since he hadn't felt anxious. When he left the Marine Corps, he thought that a job with the Secret Service would be less stressful. The demands of the job would engage him well enough, but nothing ever happened to the President. He would be able to fulfill his need for action without ever dealing with a threat more serious than a crackpot with a pipe bomb or a college student with a handgun who thought he could make himself famous.

For a long time, that had been the case. Then Bard had defected and decided he wanted to play God. The past six months had provided Jake with enough stress to last a lifetime. If the injuries he'd suffered didn't kill him, a heart attack wasn't out of the question.

It felt good to feel calm, even for a moment. He scanned the crowd with deadly precision, and if he needed to, he would kill with equal precision. Still, despite being primed for war in its most simple and brutal sense, he felt at peace.

While the crowd within one hundred fifty yards of the wall was limited to the preselected press agents, the crowd just beyond was composed of a far different sort. A great many people were there for reasons that had nothing at all to do with the President's visit. There were many that seemed, in fact, completely unaware of anyone else around them as they prayed. Though this was not an organized call to prayer, the murmuring of the crowd ebbed and flowed in near harmony. If not for the events of the day and the risk of another serious attack, their voices might be almost hypnotic.

But he couldn't allow himself to be lulled by the noise. He scanned the rest of the crowd. Beyond the supplicants, there were, of course, a great many spectators. There were the usual number of protestors as well, but Israeli Police held them a significant distance from the wall.

Interestingly enough, the protestors weren't taking sides in any conflict. They were climate protestors, college students of various nationalities who lacked the capacity to understand that the carbon burned to fly them business class from their countries of origins so they could tell people they protested the President's climate policies in Jerusalem damaged their credibility. There wasn't a threat there. Most of them were there just for social media clout. There would be press there and with any luck they would be seen briefly on television. Perhaps the news would make them seem more important to the events of the day.

He also saw no threats among the worshippers praying. There were some highly emotional individuals, of course, but there was nothing more than religious fervor involved in their wailing and weeping and the arms upthrust to the sky held no weapon but the zeal of the various faithful. Certainly, there was no evidence of the fanaticism that might lead some to act violently.

He scanned the crowd of tourists, those who were here for no particular reason but knew that the Western Wall was an important landmark according to their Welcome to Israel pamphlet. It was more difficult to decide if any of them were threatening, but nothing stood out to him.

"Eagle is on the move," Jess said in his earpiece.

"We didn't like Lion?" Jake asked.

"I did, but you insisted on using a different codename this time. You know, because you enjoy being by the book, but only when it's really annoying and serves no actual purpose."

"Huh. I wouldn't put up with me if I were you."

"Believe me, if I had a choice."

He chuckled and turned his attention back to the crowd. With no threat from the spectators, worshippers and protesters, he wasn't sure exactly where to look until he thought back to the subterfuge in Damascus with press drones. That drew his attention to the press corps. They waited expectantly, but apart from typical jockeying for position, there was nothing that…

Then there was.

As the President made his way to where he would speak, Jake saw someone suspicious. One particular reporter displayed multiple red flag behavioral cues. His eyes moved constantly, but he avoided eye contact. He appeared nervous, rocking back and forth on his feet. He checked his phone repeatedly. Jake looked at him through the scope and could see excessive perspiration. His body language didn't fit for the occasion. He seemed alternately jumpy and overly relaxed, as though he was repeatedly reminding himself to be nonchalant.

He quickly hailed Jess on the radio. "I have a potential threat," he said, "with the press."

"Who?" she asked.

"Brown blazer, blue fedora."

"Right in the front on the left side?"

"That's the one."

"All right. I'll deploy security in that direction."

"Okay, but do it quietly," he said. "I wouldn't put it past Hadad to have shills here just to distract us.

"Okay. I'll send a security task force that direction, but we'll be cautious."

And that was when chaos erupted on the scene below. At first, Jake couldn't see the actual danger. What he saw was the panicked reaction to the danger. Screaming drowned out the prayers and murmuring. Then the prayers stopped as the crowd scrambled for safety.

Then Jake saw the terrorists. They moved through the crowd, yelling and pulling handguns from places hidden on their bodies. Jake had set up metal detectors, but there were plastic guns and ceramic cartridges that could bypass those detectors.. He was right, Hadad or Bard or whoever was leading this assault was trying to cause a distraction.

He scanned the air, looking for drones, thinking that Hadad was once more planning his assault to come from somewhere unexpected while his terrorists caused a commotion. When he didn't see a threat in the air, he looked back at the crowd.

And saw a single terrorist heading purposefully toward the President.

Jake lifted his rifle and took aim. He fired, and the man went down.

He tapped his earpiece. "Dawson, what are we looking at?"

"I believe the technical term is a clusterfuck, sir. I'm working on getting the President toward tunnel… Shit!"

Jake's eyes and rifle snapped to the top of the wall to see the President's security detail pinned down by a force of terrorists. To the detail's credit, Jake couldn't see the President at all. He was completely surrounded by Secret Service Agents.

Some of whom would die protecting his right to wave his dick.

Jake forced the anger down and took aim with his rifle. It wouldn't help for him to give in to his anger right now.

He fired, then fired, then fired again. Each shot took down a terrorist, and when he fired his fifth shot, emptying his magazine, he replaced it so quickly and smoothly he was hardly aware of it.

When he looked through the scope again, the terrorists were overcome, and Dawson was leading his team through the cleared path.

Jake's earpiece crackled. "Mercer, this is Dawson."

"Go ahead, Dawson."

"Threat is neutralized, and the team is proceeding. Can you tell me which route is safest for Eagle?"

"Thirty seconds, Dawson."

He tapped his earpiece twice, then said, "Captain Yosef, what are we looking at on the ground?"

"The terrorists have begun firing on civilians," the Israeli Police leader replied. "We are coordinating evacuations, but it is brutal close-quarters combat right now. We are likely looking at triple-digit casualties."

Jake couldn't fault the man for replying from the perspective of his own country's losses. At the knowledge that—as in Washington six months ago—many civilians would succumb to the violent attack, Jake felt a pang of grief and rage himself.

But his job was to protect the President, and he needed to ask the next question. "Do you know which of the escape routes are still viable?"

He imagined the police captain was enraged at least a little knowing that Jake could so easily dismiss the loss of so many of his people, but he was spared the need to swallow that rage when Captain Topol of the IDF ground forces said, "IDF reinforcements are engaging the enemy. We will have the civilian situation under control momentarily. No three-digit casualties today, Yosef. As far as the American President, I suggest he avoid the tunnels and stay on the surface. Your Rapid Response Team is making its way to the base of the wall at Entrance Gimel. Have your president meet them there. The terrorists are very poorly trained and will not stand a chance against your forces."

"Thank you, Captain Topol."

"Jake," Jess's voice chimed in. "I've contacted Marine One. They're going to meet the President at a flat portion of the city three hundred yards north of Entrance Gimel. They're carrying a platoon of Marines with them to provide extra cover, and the Air Force will have F-35s here to provide air support before Marine One arrives."

"Outstanding."

Jake could take some comfort in the fact that they were better prepared for the terrorists this time. In one way, returning to the same place twice had turned out to be a good thing. They had adapted well to the terrorist threat. The terrorists hadn't adapted nearly so well.

And, as usual, no sooner had the words left Jake's mouth than they were proven to be premature.

Jake wasn't on the wall when the bomb exploded, but the force of it still knocked Jake off his feet. Dust peppered his eyes, and the building he was in rattled sickeningly. His ears rang, and he couldn't be sure if he managed to form the words correctly when he said, "Dawson! Report now!"

His words must have been understandable enough, because although his ears still rang with the force of the explosion, he heard Dawson's voice clearly say, "The President is alive! We made it just outside of the wall. Cole and Murphy are down. Repeat: the President is alive, Cole and Murphy are down!"

Jake sighed. More good men lost. "Do you have eyes on Marine One?"

"Yes, sir. Marine One is hovering twenty-five feet aboveground. Debris has made it impossible for them to land."

Without hesitation, Jake said, "Marine One, deploy the ladder. Evacuate the President ASAP!"

Jake tried to stand, but his balance hadn't yet returned. He fell backward, and his ears started to ring again. He gritted his teeth and forced himself to his feet, holding onto the windowsill for support.

He looked toward the wall, and through the dust caused by its collapse, he could see the Marine squad deploy from Marine One and quickly drive back the terrorists who had converged on the President's position. Dawson dragged the President to the ladder, placing his body in between the President and the terrorists, then climbed with the President, at no time providing the terrorists a target.

He was a good agent. Jake would see to it that he received a commendation.

The Marines remained below, and a few moments later, they linked up with the IDF forces. Jake waited until his head stopped swimming, then left the building. By the time he reached the ground level, the terrorists who hadn't been killed or captured were fleeing, realizing that once more, their attempt on the President's life had failed.

But they had drawn their share of blood in the effort. Jake looked around and sighed at the piles of bodies that littered the ground around the ruins of the wall. Captain Topol had promised the casualties would remain light, but that was a promise it didn't appear he could keep.

Jake tried to tell himself that this was a victory, but looking around at the dead civilians, he couldn't bring himself to feel that way.

CHAPTER FIFTEEN

Jake woke the next morning feeling surreal. The dreamlike feeling was much the same as it was the day before when the wall exploded. He thought for a moment that he might have a delayed reaction to a concussion, but when he rolled out of bed, his limbs moved easily. There was a dull ache in his midsection where he had been stabbed three months ago, but even that was far less intense than it had been. Physically, he was nearly healed, despite the more recent ravages his body had endured.

Mentally, he wasn't sure he would ever heal. The feeling he had reminded him of the morning of September 12, 2001. The attack, of course, had taken place the day before, but it hadn't seemed real to Jake until the next morning when he woke up to see the headlines discussing the attack and turned on the tv to see an image of the South Tower collapsing.

He felt now as he did then, and he imagined the Israelis felt the same. It was possible they hadn't. They had lived in a world of violence throughout the entirety of their people's history. This was a tragedy, but if there was a people on Earth hardened enough to endure tragedy, it was the Israelis.

Not that that fact made anything better. Looking around at the destruction outside still brought a pang to Jake's heart.

He flipped on the news and wasn't surprised to see that another brazen attack on the President had shaken America to its core. Americans weren't used to feeling vulnerable, even after 9/11, but the past six and a half months had made it abundantly clear to the nation that they were, in fact, vulnerable. It made it worse knowing that the threat came from inside.

Bard had escaped. The biggest victory they could possibly have hoped to achieve was no victory at all. Jake suspected that Bard had allowed himself to be captured. He had even told Jake about the attack on the wall, and still, they had come within a hairs' breadth of losing the President.

Jake shook his head. The constant threat was getting to him. In U.S. History, there were four assassinated Presidents and fourteen unsuccessful attempts. The most recent prior attempt happened to President Ronald Reagan in 1981, just a few months after his inauguration. He was shot, but his recovery made him seem invincible and heroic. That attempt wasn't even politically motivated. The assassin was insane, and thought he was impressing a film star.

Eighteen Presidents.

That was the sum total of all attempted assassinations from George Washington to the current President's predecessor. And Bryan Jackson had survived seven assassination attempts. If they couldn't neutralize Bard for good, it was possible there would be eighteen attempts on this particular Commander in Chief.

No. There wouldn't be.

Jake wasn't filled with enough hubris to believe that he could protect the President from another eleven or twelve attacks. He especially didn't believe it would be possible if the President remained stubborn. If he refused to change his plans or behaviors moving forward… Jake didn't like to think about it.

He pushed the thought from his mind. He had work to do. Today would be spent working on recovery and rescue missions. He would work with various US Embassy employees, operatives, and soldiers along with Israeli forces and first responders to coordinate search and rescue parties for American citizens trapped in the rubble. The embassy estimated there were thirty-eight missing Americans.

Most of them would end up dead. Some of them would never be found.

Jake would rather focus on tracking down Hadad, but with no lead on the man's whereabouts and the President already safe at home in D.C., there was nowhere for Jake to go. If he returned home, he would just be sitting and waiting. The FBI was leading the manhunt for Bard, and for once, the Secret Service wasn't attempting to butt into another agency's job. Helping with the recovery efforts in Jerusalem was the best use of Jake's time.

A few hours later, though, as he organized operations in the debris of the post-attack landscape, he got a call. The name on the screen surprised him. He was very happy to see it, though. "Sheila," he said as he answered. "How are you doing?"

"What matters right now is how you're doing," she replied. He thought if the measure of a relationship was each person caring more for the other's wellbeing than their own, the two of them would last.

"I'm good," he said. It wasn't entirely true, but it wasn't really a lie, either. "It's good to hear your voice."

"Well, I hope it's good to hear what I say, too," she said. "There's a lead on Hadad's location," she said, "and they're going to call you with it. Who knows when, though? I wanted to…" Her voice broke.

"You wanted to help me skip the politics," he said. "You wanted to give me the information I need before everyone gets their say about everything."

"No," she said. Her voice was thin, tremulous. She sounded on the verge of tears, and a chill ran through him.

"Baby, what happened?"

"I… I got a text."

Jake's blood froze. In addition to threats to the President, Sheila herself had been directly threatened frequently since Trident first began moving against the President. Three months ago, in Vilezy-Villacoublay, France, Vincent St. Clair—the mad scientist who had created a supervirus for Trident, had threatened to kill Sheila in front of Jake.

Jake had assigned two agents to shadow the First Daughter everywhere she went, and he'd given her a secure phone—a gift from Mr. Quartz, a CIA operative whose partner, Miss Topaz, had been instrumental in stopping St. Clair, eventually giving her life to stop him.

"On your secure phone?"

"Yes. He… they… whoever it was didn't threaten me this time, though."

Jake's brow furrowed. "What did it say?"

"It said, 'tell the rat to hunt underground.' There was no number, and… well, I guess I don't know for sure that it was meant for you, but I can't imagine what else it would be."

Jake's lips thinned. "It was meant for me. And no, strange as it is to say considering everything, I don't think it was meant to threaten you. I think Bard is taunting me."

"Do you think it's a trap?"

Jake considered that a moment. Bard had shared plenty of information on Hadad that had turned out to be accurate. He had also told Jake that Hadad was a colleague and not a subordinate, hinting that he didn't have control over Hadad. Jake knew from his experience with St. Clair that Bard didn't like people he couldn't control. Bard would no doubt have been very happy to see Bard succeed in assassinating the

President and kill Jake with him, but he might also be happy to have Jake take care of his not-subordinate problem.

It could be a trap, or it could be Bard siccing Jake on Hadad like a dog. Either way, it needed to be explored.

"I don't think so," he said to Sheila, once again not quite the truth and not quite a lie.

"Why would they be helping you?"

Jake didn't want to share too much with Sheila. It was better that she not have the details. Still, there was no lie he could think of that would sound believable.

"I can't share much," he replied, "but we believe that there's infighting within Trident. It's possible that the person who threatened you in the past is now using your phone to feed us information we can use to stop his associates."

"But I have a new phone."

"Same number, though," he said, "which we will fix immediately. Show this text to Special Agent Trent and tell him you want a secure phone with a new number. He'll set you up. He'll also beef up security for you just in case this is an implied threat. I'm fairly sure it's not meant to be a threat to you, though."

"So they're using me to get to you?"

"It's possible. I really can't say more, though. The less you know, the better."

He hated having to dismiss Sheila's feelings like this, but she was already far too involved in this. He couldn't risk putting her in any more danger.

You mean by continuing to date her while actively opposing the most dangerous domestic terrorist in the nation's history?

He felt a pang and thought for the hundredth time that it really was a mistake to have let himself fall so hard for Sheila.

But what could he do? He couldn't stop feeling the way he felt.

He recalled a conversation they'd had in France where she expressed her dream of one day leaving politics behind and moving to a cabin in the woods somewhere the two of them could live a simple and quiet life free of the dangers and intrigue of government. At the time, Jake didn't think he could ever live like that and be fulfilled. Now, he wished more than anything else that he were already in that cabin with her and that Bard and Trident and Hadad were someone else's problem.

But they weren't someone else's problem. They were his problem, and he couldn't pull back and leave the job unfinished.

He said goodbye to Sheila and called Jess. She was back in D.C. “Hey, Jake. You coming in to work today?”

“Yes, but not the same kind of work.”

“Oh?”

“We got a lead.”

He briefly outlined the information he’d gotten from Sheila. When he finished, Jess didn’t respond for a long time. When she did, her voice was hesitant. “Jake… I don’t want you to take this the wrong way, but… do you think maybe you and Sheila should wait? Not forever, just until we stop Trident. It feels like she’s never quite out of danger, and I worry that Bard might target her to get to you.”

Jake had had the same thought many times, but the answer he gave Jess was the entire truth and not at all a lie. "I think Bard would target her either way. She's the President's only child and the darling of the news media. She would be a high-value target no matter what."

Jess paused another moment before saying, not too convincingly, “All right.”

Jake pushed down the touch of guilt he felt and said, “Can you reach out to Mossad and have them put together a team for me? We’re going into the tunnels again.”

“Will do,” Jess replied. “Be careful.”

“I will,” Jake replied. “Bard forgets how resilient rats are.”

He meant the comment to be funny, but he wasn’t surprised when Jess didn’t laugh.

CHAPTER SIXTEEN

Jake wondered how many times he would be back under the tunnels of Jerusalem. "Stay alert," he said to his team.

Of course, it was impossible not to stay alert. The tunnels were all but pitch dark. Their helmet lamps gave only faint light that cast long shadows on the walls. The walls were covered with centuries of grime. He understood it was necessary. If there really were a reasonable chance Hadad hid here, they needed to be in the tunnels. Still, it seemed insane to return to the exact circumstances that almost killed his team before.

On the bright side, he was more prepared now if anything were to happen. Unless, of course, Hadad had rigged another bomb to go off to collapse the tunnels on them. Jess's scans hadn't picked anything up, but she had also been unable to determine what explosive had caused the Western Wall to collapse, so it was very possible that Hadad had some insane bleeding-edge tech developed from the data he had stolen from the DARPA bunker that Jess couldn't track.

Hell, at this point, Jake wouldn't have been surprised to see gargoyles jump out of the floor with the Trident logo stamped to their foreheads.

He reached out to touch the wall beside him. The roughhewn stone was no more ancient than the Western Wall, but they felt older somehow than anything aboveground. The eerie silence no doubt caused that impression.

No, not quite silence. It was more like a soft muting of sound, like placing a cotton ball in one's ears. He was aware of sound pressure without any sound, and that gave the tunnels an eerie sense of foreboding.

Hell, the entire place gave off a sense of foreboding. The air had a metallic tang that lingered at the back of his throat. The smell of stone and earth was overpowering, almost claustrophobic. His headlamp flickered, casting an ephemeral glow over the wall. The flickering light made it seem like there was writing or etching, but when he looked closer, he could see that what he thought was etching was only the play of light and shadow across the texture of the rock. It was simply another trick, another part of these damned tunnels' curse.

"Careful," he said, "keep your eyes open and keep your focus." His men acknowledged the command with voices as tense as his own.

He tapped his earpiece. "You have the imagery loaded, Jess? Like the last time, Jess would be their navigator. Ideally, the satellite imagery would provide their lifeline. It would be some sort of digital string to rescue them from the Minotaur in the labyrinth.

"Yes. Because I'm awesome and decided to scan the tunnels with terrain-mapping satellites."

"Awesome. Keep me posted if we end up finding enemies.

"Ahem."

Despite the tension he felt, he couldn't resist a smile. "And you are the most awesome partner in the world, and I'm lucky to breathe the same air as you."

"Better," Jess said.

Jake continued inching forward. His senses were just hyper-engaged. He could feel the soles of his combat boots compress as he lowered is foot and push off of the floor as he raised it. He could hear his breath filling his lungs, feel them contract as he exhaled. A soft breeze blew through the tunnels, the last gasp of a far stiffer breeze on the surface, He could feel it move the hairs on the back of his hands.

He continued moving forward with halting progress. Every step felt like a small, laborious victory. The air seemed oppressive. Everything about the damned tunnels seemed oppressive.

As they delved deeper, it would get worse. He was certain of that. He hated being underground.

"Still got visual?" Jake queried into his radio again. He knew she did. He just wanted to break the silence.

"Don't worry about me. I got you covered. You hanging in there?"

"Barely," he admitted. "I have a thing about caves ever since Paris."

"I know," she said gently. "Don't worry, all right. You'll be… Oh shit, Jake! Hostiles ahead!"

The tunnels opened into a cavern. And then gunfire exploded around him.

"Down!" he shouted, diving to the ground. He immediately fired in the direction of the muzzle flashes, noting with gratification that a large number of his men did the same. He inched forward, firing continuously. If Hadad's soldiers hadn't learned from the last battle, the suppressive fire would give Jake and his team some help here.

There were only scattered muzzle flashes now. "Flares!" Jake called. He heard the torch-like sound of one and then another. He focused his eyes ahead as he heard a third. Simultaneously, the first two flares flew forward. The flares allowed Jake to see the outlines of five or six hostiles. He fired and took out one immediately. His second shot hit home. He didn't know if the shot was lethal, but his third shot definitely was. The terrorist who'd been shot let out a blood-curdling scream that was quickly silenced when a Mossad bullet tore out his throat.

The Mossad team was far better prepared for this assault than they were the last time they were underground. Every burst fired was effective, and the muzzle flashes of their enemy grew more and more sporadic.

He didn't have any opportunity to celebrate, though. A second wave of hostiles approached, and Jake realized there were more of Hadad's soldiers here than last time. He didn't know if these ones were better trained, but as the third flare flew across the cavern, only a few still stood. The rest were taking cover. He downed one of those standing, and his men got the others.

"We can't stay here, Jess," he radioed.

"I got you," she said, "You want to go deeper in, or do you want out of the tunnels?"

"I'm not leaving the tunnels with nothing to show for it," Jake said. "There are more of them this time, but their tactics haven't improved. If this is a trap, it's a poor one, but I'm thinking there's no trap. I think we're getting closer."

"I'll guide you in further," Jess said, "but Jake, something just occurred to me. Hadad's a weapons dealer. He's made a point out of *not* having soldiers in his employ but only selling. It's possible that he's trying to make the transition to terrorist, but I wouldn't rule out Trident trap just yet."

"I haven't ruled it out," Jake replied, "but I have a hunch that this is another St. Clair situation. He was just a biochemist, but he ended up with a cadre of soldiers too. He also ended up on Bard's bad side."

"You think Bard gave us honest advice when he was in captivity?"

"I think so. I'm sure he won't shed a tear if Hadad ends up taking us out along with him, but I think we can trust… well, trust might be a strong word. The point is, I'm pretty sure this is a good lead."

“Well, then lay on, Macduff.”

“What?”

“Seriously? You’ve never read Macbeth?”

“Yeah, in high school.”

“God, why in the hell is the President’s daughter dating you? You’re like Lady Chatterley’s lover.”

“If that’s another Shakespeare reference, it’s completely lost on me.”

"Clearly. Anyway, at the far end of the cavern, you'll find three different tunnels. They all lead to the same place, but take the left one. There's less room there, which means less cover for the baddies. Less cover for you, too, but when the odds are even, I favor you guys."

“Sounds good.”

Jake led his men forward. The few remaining defenders in the cavern turned tail, but none made the tunnels before they were gunned down. Jake stationed two men on either side of the center and right tunnels with instructions to radio Jake if the enemy advanced. The worst thing that could happen right now would be for the enemy to flank them and trap them in a bottlenecked tunnel.

As Jess had said, the tunnel was narrow and devoid of cover. Jake and his men advanced slowly, and firing was difficult with only Jake and three or so of the agents behind him able to fire without risking hitting one of their own.

Fortunately, Jess’s gamble proved to be correct. The terrorists were not nearly as well-trained as the Mossad agents, and they reacted poorly to the claustrophobic circumstances. As many terrorists fell to friendly fire as to fire from Jake’s team. Finally, a slightly more intelligent example of a violent terrorist made the prudent choice to call for a retreat. Jake radioed for the four men he left behind to rejoin the main force on the double.

“Where to next, Jess?”

“That tunnel widens in a moment, but you’ll want to take the first narrow split to your right. It’s not as narrow as the first one, but it’s a fairly steep downhill grade, let’s see... fifteen percent.”

“Understood.”

Jake informed the team of the changing terrain and led them down the narrow tunnel. The enemy arrived shortly after, this time from behind them. Jake heard a cry from the rearmost Mossad agent, who, in Vietnam War Long Range Reconnaisance Patrol style walked backward to identify just such a threat.

Positioning the agent that way saved his life and likely the lives of several other agents. Jake turned, but from his position, he could only see glimpses of the fight ahead. The tunnel wasn't as narrow as the last one, but it was narrow enough that Jake didn't have a good shot without a strong chance of hitting one of his own men.

"Jess, where was the heads up on these guys?" Jake asked.

"I can't see infrared anymore," Jess replied. "I can still track you and your team via satellite signal, but if there are hostiles at this depth, their heat signatures are too scattered for the satellites to pick them up. I can see the tunnels, but I can't see if anything's waiting there."

"Wonderful," Jake said.

Then, a bullet buzzed past his ear and shattered the skull of the Mossad agent in front of him. Jake swore and dropped to the ground, twisting and firing as he did. The rearmost agents who couldn't fire forward did the same, and the enemy advance slowed.

It didn't stop, though. The pincer movement that Jake was afraid of had occurred, and the terrorists knew this was their best chance at stopping the team. They fought with unbridled tenacity, several of them continuing through mortal wounds, not releasing their triggers until their last breaths stole the remnants of their strength.

Earlier, the terrorists had been unable to stop the Mossad advance. Now, they pressed Jake and his team to their limits. Jake heard first one cry, then another, as terrorist bullets found their targets.

"Fall back!" Jake said. "Take cover!"

The team did as ordered, and finally, they were able to turn the tide of battle back the other way. The enemy did well against a mobile assault team, but against an entrenched one, the gaps in their training showed. They poked their heads around corners, and a few even rushed the team.

Jake fired carefully, ensuring that each bullet counted. His team did the same, and as the terrorist's numbers dwindled, their confidence waned.

Finally, as before, they broke into a run. Jake's team started after them, but Jake called for caution. "Don't rush them! Take who you can now! We'll get the rest later!"

So saying, he fired, striking a terrorist in the back. The man shrieked, then fell forward and lay still.

Jake and his team continued forward, but no more assailants awaited them. Their victory hadn't come without cost, though. They entered the tunnel with fifteen agents and Jake, but two more fell in addition to the one who had been killed earlier, and when the terrorists finally broke free and ran, they dropped two more by launching a volley of suppressive fire.

That left ten agents to leave the tunnels. They couldn't sustain those kinds of losses. "Jess, how much further?"

"One hundred yards. This time, I can tell you that the next cavern—the big one—is only seven feet lower than your position and the ground slopes gradually downward to get there. No more surprise holes or ladders."

"That's good to hear. Still no sign of enemies?"

"I still can't see them if that's what you mean."

Jake sighed. "All right. Well, we'll keep doing our best, but if we run into more trouble like the last tunnel, we'll have to abort."

"Understood. Your survival is more important than anything else."

Jake wasn't sure he agreed with that, but he wouldn't get the rest of the Mossad agents killed chasing a miracle.

Fortunately, the terrorists they had defeated showed no sign of returning, and they reached the next cavern unmolested.

The moment Jake's lamp illuminated the cavern, he knew he had found his goal. Rather than the one isolated terminal in the middle of a natural cave, this cavern had been built out into an extensive and advanced underground lair. There were rows of computer terminals, stacks of weapons, some of them easily recognizable and others so strange that Jake couldn't even be sure there were weapons.

"Jake? What do you see?"

Jake tapped his earpiece. "I think I see Hadad's headquarters.

CHAPTER SEVENTEEN

The team quickly sifted through the base, opening filing cabinets and cracking into terminals. The file cabinets were empty and the terminals were protected by sophisticated firewalls, but when they attached thumb drives loaded with firewall cracking software directly to the servers, they were able to confirm that Hadad hadn't had time to wipe any of the data. Evidently, Jake's team's arrival underground had startled Hadad. The resistance they encountered in the tunnels was likely to cover Hadad's escape.

He had made his escape, but he had left behind a treasure trove of data.

If only they could access it.

"No good," Special Agent Zohan said to Jake, looking away from his laptop which was currently attached to one of the servers. "The data is encrypted. It could take weeks to decode it."

"We don't have weeks," Jake replied.

"I know," Zohan said. "Perhaps if we download the data and send it to Mossad and NSA headquarters, they can access it faster."

"I'll do you one better," Jake said. He tapped his earpiece. "Jess, I'm sending you some data from Hadad's servers here on the base. See if you can crack through it."

"Understood," Jess replied. "Three eggs sunny side up, coming your way."

"What?"

"You know, because you crack eggs."

"Why sunny side up?"

"Because that's the only way any egg should ever be eaten."

He shrugged. "I prefer mine poached."

Jess paused a second. "Well, you've been hit on the head a lot recently. I'll chalk it up to severe brain damage."

He chuckled and said, "All right, chef, focus on the data, and when I get home, I'll make you a poached egg so good you'll forget all about sunny side up."

"Better not tell Sheila you're making me breakfast."

"What?"

“Never mind. Are you planning on sending that data today, or what?”

Jake chuckled and took the thumb drive from Zohan. He plugged it into his phone and said, “All right, Jess, it’s on his way.”

While the data was uploaded, Jake looked around the base. It was truly impressive, but it was also a touch haphazard. The rows of terminals were stationed far away from the servers, trailing thick ropes of cables behind them. The servers themselves were piled together rather than stacked together with any kind of order, and the unfinished weapons left behind appeared to have been hand-assembled with simple tools. They looked functional, or rather like they would be functional if they were completed, but they were far from the sophisticated drones Hadad had used in his first two attacks.

That was more evidence that they were getting to him. Then he realized there was probably a simple answer to that. “Hey, Jess, when we interrogated Mahmoud about money, did we freeze his accounts?”

“We? No, honey, *I* froze his accounts. Thanks for finally noticing, like, ten years later.”

Jake chuckled. “All right. I owe you two poached eggs.”

“You owe me whatever I… Oh God.”

Jake’s smile instantly vanished at the alarm in Jess’s voice. “Jess? What is it?”

Jess's voice came in low, barely a whisper. He strained to hear her. "I cracked the code. Hadad doesn't want wars, Jake."

"What are you talking about? All that stuff we got from the thumb drive at his old base was fake?"

"No. Not fake. I just mean he's not looking at generic conflict and unrest. He specifically wants America and the Middle East to go head-to-head, full-blown."

Jake's was quiet for a moment. He hadn't expected this. He knew there would be U.S. involvement, of course. It wasn't possible to have wars in the Middle East without it. But now, Hadad's plan went beyond war profiteering and weapons smuggling. "He wants to arm U.S. enemies," Jake said. “H’s playing off of the tension between the U.S. and the Arab world.”

"Yes," Jess replied. "Multiple conflicts between as many nations as possible and the U.S. More buyers for his weapons. The best way to do that is to light a spark under the barrel of dynamite."

It made sense. The United States had enemies all across the globe, but the Middle East was unique in that nearly all of the regional powers there had been involved in direct conflicts with the U.S. Most of the conflicts had been small regional skirmishes, at least from the U.S. perspective, but violence wasn't something to be postured here as it often was in other regions. It was something taken with deadly seriousness. If Hadad could…

Oh God.

"Is he trying to attack the Middle East with U.S. weapons? Trying to make them think that we've gone off the rails and are trying to commit regional genocide?"

"Would you believe me if I said it was worse than that?"

Jake's heart sank even further. He hated every word of the next question that escaped his lips. "How could it possibly be worse?"

"He wants to attack the United States with advanced weaponry. He wants to convince the United States that our enemies in the Middle East actually have the capacity to hurt us."

"Advanced weapons," Jake said. "Made using the plans he stole from the bunker."

"Yes."

Jake was fiercely grateful now for the evidence that, at least for now, Hadad didn't have the resources to accomplish that goal.

"We're dealing with a madman here, Jake," Jess said.

Jake wished he could agree with that, but he couldn't. The plan was sound. Incredibly sound. If the U.S. attacked a Middle Eastern nation, the result would be the same as they'd seen in the past. The U.S. would very quickly and decisively destroy the standing military forces of whatever nation they deemed responsible, then sit a large occupational force inside that nation's territory. They would face attritional warfare from guerillas and insurgents, but there would be no possibility of an organized response.

That was usually how arms dealers made their money. They sold small to moderate quantities of weapons to guerillas and freedom fighters and profited off of long-term, low-scale conflicts.

But if the United States was convinced that a nation—worse, a coalition of nations—from the Middle East had the ability to cause serious damage to the United States, then the U.S. response would be unparallelled. A regional skirmish involving an expeditionary force would become a full-scale war involving the entire might of the U.S. military.

And it would be brutal. The U.S. was not in the business of terrorizing civilian populations, but when it came to their own national sovereignty and security, especially in a post-9/11 world, they weren't always careful. In a case where they believed that sovereignty and security were seriously threatened, they would be even less careful.

There would be outcries. There would be protests. Some of those protests would result in hotheads and idiots pressing buttons they shouldn’t press, and those isolated attacks would lead to brutal retaliation. The fighting would quickly spill over throughout the region, and in a case like that, governments of nations with fierce pride but the intelligence to recognize that they stood no chance against the full might of the United States would be all too happy to pay any price for weapons like the ones Hadad now knew how to manufacture.

And Hadad would be there to reap the rewards. Part of Jake wondered if that was why Bard had turned on Hadad. Bard wanted to overthrow the United States government, but while he clearly had no trouble hurting civilians to accomplish that goal, he definitely didn’t want to risk destroying the country he hoped to run.

"The problem," Jake said, "is that we're not dealing with a madman. We're dealing with someone rational but... Rational but evil."

"Is that better?"

"It’s worse. Far worse. We need to determine a course of action. To do that, we need more information. Hell, we need *all* the information: where Hadad is, where he’s going, what resources he has access to, where, when and how he plans to manufacture his weapons, his targets and timeline… everything. We need the man’s damned grocery list.”

"I know I'm just the computer nerd," Jess said, "but it seems to me that you're right where you need to be to get that information."

"Exactly," Jake said. He called, "Gather 'round!"

His words echoed off the cavern walls, reverberating ominously through the still nearly-silent tunnels. The members of his team converged on him. Soon, they formed a circle of faces half hidden in shadow. "All right, everyone," Jake said, "we have good intelligence about Hadad's plans, but we need more. We need to fine-toot this place. We need fresh intelligence. We need more insight into Hadad's operations. Get me something."

The team nodded acknowledgment and split up. They worked with a sense of urgency, and Jake could swear he felt the temperature drop a few degrees.

The near-silence of the place grew more oppressive. The only sounds he heard came from his breathing and the footsteps his team made. He almost engaged with Jess on the radio just to hear something different.

"Paper," someone said, a welcome break to the silence. "Lots of paper." He looked around. It took a moment for his eyes to adjust to the darkness. Once he had, though, he could see one of the men down on one knee looking through a box. It looked like Hadad hadn't made it out with all of his files after all.

In very short order, it became apparent that the papers represented a gold mine of new information. They found receipts and ledgers with detailed accounts of past arms deals. They found strategic plots planned but abandoned, along with brainstormed notes for new plans.

The sheer volume of it was overwhelming. Hadad wasn't just supplying arms. He was playing puppet master, creating a show of chaos. The picture of Hadad as an over-the-top, maniacal supervillain was really beginning to take form for Jake.

Hadad hadn't become a terrorist. He had always been one. He just hadn't shown his face until Bard nudged him.

Jake sighed. Once more, he had to consider the possibility that Bard knew exactly what he was doing. He might want Hadad to be stopped, but then, he might not want Hadad to be stopped until he had done serious damage to the United States.

For the thousandth time, Jake longed for the day when Bard was either dead or captured—truly captured—and locked in a box at a CIA facility the public would never know about.

"There's a lot of intelligence on military operations here," an agent said. "I don't mean his own military operations. I mean, he's collected intelligence about operations in the area. It's extensive."

Jake skimmed the files the agent had examined and saw that they were indeed extensive. The detail and organization of the reports was more than a simple arms dealer or even a not-so-simple terrorist mastermind could have come up with. Perhaps Hadad had a background in intelligence. It would explain his ability to break into the bunker successfully.

"Outstanding work," Jake said, "let's see what else we can figure out."

"Right away, Sir."

He tapped his earpiece. "Jess, we found—"

He stopped when he heard signs of a struggle. At first, his brain tried to tell his ears that there was no way they could possibly be hearing what they were hearing. Jess was safe. She was home, in D.C. No one was out there who could get to her.

Then Jess screamed, "Dalton!" and Jake knew the truth of it.

Terrifying as the sounds of a struggle were, the sound of the satellite feed cutting off, leaving Jake in an even more oppressive silence than before, was worse.

"Jess!" he cried. "Jess!"

There was no answer.

Jake resisted the urge to sink to his knees as the walls of the cavern closed in around him.

CHAPTER EIGHTEEN

Jake took a breath and fought down panic. He tried to call headquarters to alert them about the danger to Jess, but there was no cell connection and when he switched to satellite, he got no signal as well. Evidently, Jess was using satellites that weren't connected to his phone, only to her computers back at headquarters.

He was about to lose his fight against panic when his phone chimed. Jess. She had sent them a map of the tunnels with four different routes highlighted that could take them to the surface.

He couldn't tell if they were a last heroic act before losing consciousness or if she had programmed the computer to send them the messages in the event her vital signs were disrupted. Or maybe she had been rescued but chosen to maintain radio silence. He hoped like hell that was the case, but he doubted it. If she could text maps, she could text him that she was all right.

She wasn't all right. Dalton had gotten to her, and whether or not he was working for Bard or acting on his own, there was no doubt that she was in life-threatening danger.

If she wasn't already dead.

Rage surged through him, but he calmed himself and looked over the map.

"Switch to radio communication," he called to his team. When the team had all acknowledged the move to radio communication, he said, "We're leaving now. Leave everything you can't easily carry and follow me."

He led them through route four. This route would take them through entirely different tunnels than the ones they had entered. It was a gamble, since those tunnels could be filled with terrorists, but Jake believed the terrorists were more likely to try to attack the team through the tunnels they had entered.

God, he hoped he was right.

"You see a hostile fire at will. They exist, they die. We clear?"

The response was unanimous. "Clear."

Jake was concerned at first that he wouldn't be able to read the map well enough to lead the team out of the tunnel, but he found it far easier to understand Jess's instructions than he expected. If Jess were hurt, she'd proven her worth once again before succumbing to the enemy. Jake reminded himself that she deserved to hear that every now and again. She was a critical part of the team even if he got all the accolades. People tended to pin medals on gunfighters, but it was the pioneers who built the west, though. Jake could fire a weapon, and he could go to war. Jess could handle the things that made America worth going to war to protect.

Jake let out a low whistle. He had never been so terrified for anyone in his life, except for when St. Clair held Sheila captive in Paris. He clicked the radio a few times to see if she would respond. Nothing. He considered calling her name verbally, but he didn't want to speak, not without knowing who might hear whatever he said. He sighed and pulled up his phone. He still couldn't get a signal.

He didn't want to text Jess for the same reason he didn't want his voice to come over the radio. He doubted anything would go through if he did, since Jess was the one in control of the satellites they were using to communicate, but he didn't want to risk that any of his communications could be intercepted and used against the team.

So, he thumbed a text to Sheila instead. It really didn't make sense to contact her. She was a civilian, and she was under his protection, not part of his team. He chose her because communicating with her brought him comfort. When he was stressed, she was like a blanket to him, a security blanket.

And that was unfair to her. She was a civilian. He was military. Technically, he was civilian too, but he wasn't really. The Secret Service—especially those agents trained for security or for the Rapid Response Teams—trained as extensively as elite military units, and since the first Trident attack on the Lincoln Memorial six and a half months ago, Jake had operated more like a Delta Force agent than a Secret Service Agent.

And she was off limits. He was responsible for eliminating threats to the President. She was the President's daughter. The only thing that could cause a greater conflict of interest than their relationship would be if Bard actually did turn him.

But he sent the text anyway. It killed him to know that he was involving her even more in a life she had made clear she wanted no part of, but he couldn't help himself.

Perhaps this was a sign of his psychological injuries. The throbbing in his midsection, which had now grown too powerful not to notice, was a sign of the physical damage he had sustained fighting Bard. Perhaps his inability to separate his personal life from his professional life was proof that his mind had suffered as much as his body.

God, he was all over the place. Jess's capture had affected him badly, underlying psychological damage or no. He needed to focus if they were going to get out of here alive.

He looked at his screen. There was no indication that the text had been delivered. Part of him hoped it hadn't. It could do nothing but worry Sheila needlessly.

Then a more horrible thought occurred to him. If Sheila tried to act on the text, she could put herself in danger. He believed that Bard had sent the last message to Sheila's phone only because he had no better way of contacting Jake. He believed that at the time, she meant Sheila no harm but wanted to push Jake to go after Hadad for him, but in light of everything he had learned at the base he wasn't so sure anymore. In any case, if Sheila actively opposed Bard, there was no question she would become a target.

He swiped back to the maps. Zohan leaned closer to look at them with him.

"We're going forward about a half-kilo. Then, we head north until we're forced to head west. If Hadad is going to attack us, The northward tunnel is where it will happen. I want everyone locked and loaded when we hit that turn."

"Yes, Sir."

Zohan relayed that information to the rest of the team. Jake glanced at his screen again and felt another pang when he thought of Jess. If he learned that she had sacrificed her life to get them this information, he would make it his mission to make Hadad and Bard pay in full.

Not just them either. Drew, Dalton, Mahmoud—everyone who had fallen to Trident's cause would be punished for hurting the people he cared about. Dalton would wish he had never given Bard the time of day.

Jake took a breath and checked his weapon. He wished he had his rifle, but the long-barreled sniper's weapon would be a poor choice for the close quarters and low visibility of the cavern.

Despite carrying only a handgun, Jake took comfort in the loaded chamber. The Glock he carried was the standard issue Secret Service weapon, but Jake had ordered custom magazines that offered a twenty-four-round capacity in a staggered double stack rather than the standard fifteen-round single stack magazine. He carried five magazines total, the one in the gun and four spares on his belt. That gave him one hundred twenty rounds. He had expended three of his magazines on the way here, which left him with forty-eight rounds.

It would have to be enough.

Trouble came ahead of the bend, before Jake anticipated it. Jake saw a slight, almost invisible flash of light. “Nine o’clock!” he shouted.

The Mossad agents laid down a volley of cover fire as they were trained to do. Instantly, muzzle flashes exploded from a few alcoves in the walls not shown in Jess’s maps.

Two of his agents fell, but Jake saw far more terrorists fall. Jake felt a touch of self-disgust at the satisfaction he felt when each terrorist died, but only a touch. These men were mass murderers, and they intended to be mass murderers on a scale not seen since the Vietnam War. It was no loss to the world that they would breathe their last in the tunnels underneath Jerusalem. Maybe that was a brutal way to think, but that didn't make it untrue.

One more Mossad agent fell, but the terrorists had quickly been decimated. They broke cover and fled, screaming, down the tunnel.

"Flares!" he shouted. "I don't want one of these assholes to get away!"

That was anger speaking and not strategy. When Jake thought of this engagement later, he would chastise himself repeatedly for allowing emotion to overcome rational thought. He would resolve not to let emotions control him.

Later.

“Not one!” he shouted again. “Not a damned one!”

The flares lit the tunnel, and as quickly as they illuminated enemy targets, those targets fell.

Zohan cried out, but when Jake turned to check on him, the Mossad agent switched his rifle to his other shoulder and said, “Minor injury! I’m fine!”

That was the last injury a member of Jake's team suffered. The resistance from the terrorists grew more and more sporadic, and when they turned west and saw a light stream into the tunnel from the exit, there were no more enemies in their way.

The team cheered when they reached the surface, but their cheers were short-lived. As they looked around and congratulated each other, they realized that only half of them had made it out. Eight of their comrades lay dead underground. They shared grim looks with Jake, who felt his own anger recede as the soberness of their sacrifice settled on him.

He opened his mouth to thank the Mossad agents and offer condolences and praise for their brave comrades, but before he could, his earpiece buzzed. “Jake! Special Agent Mercer! Come in!”

The voice was Art’s. He tapped his earpiece and said, “Art, it’s Jake. Where’s Jess? Is she all right?”

“She’s in a hospital,” Art replied, “She’s hurt, but she’ll live. It looks like her attacker tried to hack into her computer to steal data.”

“Did he succeed?”

“We’re looking into it now. It’s hard to tell. Jess has done a lot to this equipment to make it other than standard. We’ll have to talk to her about sharing some of the equipment specs with us so we don’t run into this emergency again, but that’s not important right now. What’s important is that there’s been another terrorist assault near the ruins of the Western Wall.”

“*Another* one? For Christ’s sake, does this guy have something against Israel?”

“Well, he knows you’re there, so it’s a good bet he’s trying to get to you. U.S. and Israeli forces are engaging him, but Hadad seems to have recruited a number of Syrian and Palestinian mercenaries to assist him. It’s a stalemate right now.”

“Can we call in air support?”

“In the middle of Jerusalem? Hell no.”

Jake cursed. “All right. I’ll head that way and see what I can do.”

"Be careful, Mercer. We're reasonably sure you're a high-value target to him."

“Between you and me, sir, I truly hope he finds me.”

“Spoken like a true Marine. Now kick ass like one.”

Jake smiled. “Ooh rah, sir.”

“One of these days, you’ll have to tell me what that means.”

“You wouldn’t get it. Marines only.”

Art chuckled. “Fair enough.”

Jake tapped his earpiece to cut off the connection, then turned to the Mossad agents.

“Men, it looks like Hadad wants round three. Anyone looking to take some revenge?”

As expected, all seven of the surviving agents were very eager for revenge.

“Outstanding.”

The team rushed toward the Western Wall. Jake's abdomen throbbed, and his breath came in ragged gasps, but his eyes were sharp, and his pace never slowed.

You want me, Hadad? Come get me.

CHAPTER NINETEEN

Once again, Jake approached the Western Wall. Once again, he noted with surprise the great many people there. The portion of the wall that had been destroyed by Hadad's bomb was cordoned off, of course, but the rest of the wall—at least the portion in front of it—seemed open for business.

There were locals going about their daily business, of course. Vendors. Even tour guides, though what they hoped to show people with every entrance to the wall blocked off, he didn't know. Others just walking through the area. There were a number of people praying at the wall. Jake imagined that number would never diminish.

He was struck once more by the resilience of the Israeli people. Less than seventy-two hours ago, there had been a terrorist attack and a gunfight, but they continued about their business as though this was simply a matter of course.

The Mossad team looked around in confusion. Jake felt the same. He tapped his earpiece. "Art? You said there was fighting at the Western Wall. I'm here at the wall with a team of Mossad agents, and I don't see anything."

"You don't see anything? I got a report that an Army company was engaging hostiles just in front of the wall."

"Army? There's no Army here. The Marines were deployed while the President was here, but they left when the President returned home. There might still be a few at the nearby IDF base, but they are most definitely not here."

Art swore. "Dammit. That was a false tip. Either Hadad lured you to him so he could ambush you, or he lured you away from him so he could launch an attack somewhere else."

"Or so he could escape," Jake replied. "See if you can get some real intel. I'll look around here and see what I can find."

He gave instructions to his team to split up and search the area. "Radio ASAP if you find anything. Do *not* engage without my direct orders."

The Mossad agents, clearly miffed at being duped by Hadad, agreed with a touch of reluctance. They fanned out into the crowd and quickly disappeared, their intelligence training giving them an almost uncanny ability to blend in.

Jake headed toward the wall.

He saw a large number of security personnel, particularly near the damaged portion of the wall. That brought him a measure of reassurance. He would have felt better, though, with more than what he saw. If a company of soldiers or a platoon of Marines wanted to show up, Jake wouldn't have minded. Hell, he wouldn't have minded one of the Secret Service's RRTs. The security here was IDF, but Jake didn't know how much training they had received. Often, IDF security guards were citizens serving their mandatory two years and not career soldiers. It was possible that recent events had inspired the IDF to staff the wall with crack troops, but it was just as possible that the IDF had chosen to reserve their crack troops for a manhunt or a rapid response force in case of an attack elsewhere in Jerusalem.

Still, it would have been nice to see some friendly firepower.

He would have felt much better with a gameplan, too. The security served as guards, just there. Just looking around. Just being seen. Everyone appeared completely oblivious to the danger at hand. That was good. It was also bad. What he needed was to see someone not oblivious. He needed to see someone acting suspicious, someone who could lead him to Hadad.

He said quietly into his radio. "Blend in with the crowd and keep your eyes open for anything suspicious. Keep your eyes open for Hadad. I'm going to find a vantage point." He looked longingly at the building where he'd positioned himself with his sniper rifle before. It felt like months ago. Once again, it occurred to him that there was no way for him or for anyone to keep calm under these circumstances. Attacks on the President were supposed to be ridiculously infrequent.

Save the planet from this.

Save the planet from that.

Protect the free world from this evil.

Protect the whole world from that evil.

Most heroic people did one or two heroic things in their whole lives. War heroes became war heroes from single battles. Famous prosecutors took down one criminal organization. Famous lawmen took down one major criminal. Movie franchises made it seem like every hero had an endless capacity for this sort of thing, but real-life heroes tended not to last past their one trial.

Jake wasn't sure how long he could keep this up. His abdomen ached. His body was on the verge of exhaustion. He was in far better shape than he had been when the President left for Syria two weeks ago and his condition had improved by light years from the near-death he had experienced in France, but as Jess was fond of reminding him, he wasn't a hundred percent yet.

Jess. Now Jess had suffered injuries too. She would live, but she was hurt. Art hadn't told him how hurt. If she had to suffer like him…

He sighed. There would come a time when he was just empty of ability and strength. There would come a time when he was empty of energy. Maybe that's what Bard wanted. Maybe all of this was just his way of weakening Jake and all of the others who stood in his way until when the time came, he could simply brush them aside.

Well, that time hadn't arrived yet. "Status reports," he said softly into the radio.

Reports came back as team members reported their positions. They blended seamlessly with the crowd. Jake could see them, but that was only because he knew where to look and what to look for. He waited for three more status reports. After two minutes or so, he heard the last report. "Holding position twenty-five meters southwest of the blanket vendor."

Jake looked in that direction. It seemed garish and offensive for vendors to be here so soon after so many had died. Then again, Jake had never been poor. Perhaps they had no choice but to sell, even if the ground on which they stood was still stained with the blood of their countrymen.

A number of stone cells along the southwest corner of the wall as well as some across the street were called Herodian Shops. They were mostly open and, after the bombing, in ruins. Jake had carefully examined them as potential points of weakness for security. They didn't provide enough cover to really represent a threat upon closer inspection, however.

None of the current vendors with their blankets, food, trinkets, and souvenirs occupied one of the ancient shops. Instead, they stood almost defensively behind tables. They called tourists and guards alike. They treated anyone who came without twenty-five yards as a customer. They did all they could to draw them in. Jake imagined that aspect of life here hadn't changed much since ancient times.

The area was alive with the aroma of spice and olives emanating from the many food vendors peppered around the area. If Jake hadn't been here when it happened, he could almost believe that no attack had taken place at all.

Jake scanned the crowd for a few moments longer and then reached for his radio to give additional instructions. As he brought it to his face, though, his eyes scanned a camera vendor. He quickly turned his attention back.

It was him.

Hadad.

He wore a tourist hat and a tourist tee-shirt, things sold from a rack next to his cameras. He wasn't disguised much except that his outfit and demeanor were the exact opposite of how he ordinarily looked. In all known images of Hadad, he wore an expensive and perfectly tailored suit.

Still, there was no mistaking the arrogant smile or the calculating eyes.

Jake might have rushed him right then, but he noticed the man rested his hand on a black box with at least one dial and two flip switches.

Jake would have given anything for his rifle right now. It would be so simple to raise and fire and take Hadad out before the man even knew he was there. From this distance, he wasn't confident he could make an accurate shot with his handgun.

Then Jake's eyes widened. That's exactly what he could do. Not him personally, but only moments ago, he had thought of how skilled the Mossad agents were at blending in.

He knew from many stories told him by Max and other Marine veterans along with CIA and other Secret Service agents that they were just as adept at killing people unseen.

He stopped in front of a fruit vendor and pretended to be interested in a small sack of pomegranates. The proprietor, thankfully, was in the middle of closing a sale with another guest and didn't have time to talk to Jake yet.

Jake tapped his earpiece and said, "Tourist outfit, t-shirt and hat, near a disposable camera vendor ninety yards from the north end of the wall."

A moment later, Zohan's voice said, "We have him. Is that our guy?"

"That's him. Be quiet and calm. He has a device in his right hand that might be a detonator. We need that detonator secured, and we need

Hadad taken down before he realizes he's being stalked. Feel free to kill him. I don't want to risk he has some kind of backup detonator."

"Understood. We'll close in on him."

Jake set the pomegranate down and walked away before he could be accosted by the proprietor. Then it occurred to him that he couldn't simply linger here. He approached another vendor, this one a seller of jewelry made from what was clearly shards of glass but advertised as gemstones from the River Jordan.

He allowed the seller to "dupe" him into spending forty dollars on three pieces of oddly-shaped glass with aluminum chains and moved on to listen to a tour guide lecture about the history of the wall. As he meandered, he watched Zohan and three other agents close in on the unsuspecting Hadad.

They nearly had him. They were so close. Just a few more yards. A few more feet.

Then Hadad just happened to look his way. It was a freak accident. Jake was over forty yards from him. There were at least eighty people in between the two of them.

But Hadad's eyes met his own, and in that split second, Jake knew they had been recognized.

Hadad's eyes widened. He turned to run.

In a flash, Zohan's arm reached out and snatched the detonator from his grasp. If Hadad had tried to retrieve it, he would have been killed by Zohan's knife, but instead, he kept running, and when the crowd realized what was happening, a very understandable panic ensued. Hadad had a head start, and he used it well. He was going to evade the Mossad agents.

Jake cursed and sprinted after Hadad. His injury stung in sharp, rhythmic pulses, and his body shook with pins and needles, a remnant of nerve damage left behind by the virus he had suffered from in Paris.

But he ran. As before, he would die if it came to it.

He ran, but Hadad had a head start that was too great to overcome. Jake watched in impotent rage as Hadad disappeared from view in the panicked crowd.

His earpiece buzzed. "I take back all the grief I gave you about working through injury."

Jess's voice was probably the only thing that could have brought him joy at that moment. "Jess! You're all right!"

"Well, I wouldn't say that. But I'm awake, and since that's the new standard for working, I'm working. And do you know why you love me?"

"You're an excellent kisser?"

"You wish you knew how good of a kisser I was. But no, you love me because I can track Hadad. I went ahead and traced the electronic device he's carrying. I'll tell you exactly where to go and what to do. You have to just listen to mama, and everything will be okay."

Jake laughed. "Wow. You're on some good drugs, aren't you?"

"Oh God, it's wonderful. I'll share some with you when you get back."

"Sounds good. In the meantime, if he's still carrying an electronic device, I'd like to confiscate it before he uses it to blow up more of Jerusalem."

"Sounds good. Proceed forward for two hundred yards, then take your first left down the alley."

"On my way."

"Jake?"

"Yes?"

"*When* you get back. Not if. Got it?"

He smiled again. "I got it."

"Good. Now go kill that son of a bitch."

"That's the plan."

CHAPTER TWENTY

Jake pursued Hadad through the alleyways of Jerusalem for ten minutes before the terrorist emerged onto a crowded boulevard on the other side of the Wall. Incredibly, he continued back toward the wall. His detonator probably had limited range.

Dammit, they needed to stop him soon. If he reached the detonator's range before Jake could stop him, then he would destroy more of the wall and kill who knows how many people.

He reached up to tap his earpiece and order his team to start evacuating the civilians, but there were too many. Even a massive, organized response would take at least a half hour to accomplish. He didn't have that time.

Instead, he tapped his earpiece. "Zohan. He's on the other side of the wall. Can you get to us?"

Zohan swore. "Not quickly. Dammit, we're at least ten minutes from you."

Jake looked back at Hadad to see him reach into his pocket. Too late.

"Get here as soon as you can," he said.

Then he rushed forward. Hadad pulled a box similar to the first detonator from his hand. He began to move his thumb over the first of the two switches.

And Jake tackled him to the ground.

The crowd around them was thicker than the first crowd. Only a few people noticed the fight and since both men were in civilian-looking attire—Jake wore body armor, but the coat and pants he wore were a drab brown and not camo or "federal black"—the only reaction anyone gave was an irritable remark and a few laughs.

Hadad got to his feet and rushed away from the wall toward the alley he had just left. Jake rushed forward, grunting through the worsening pain and tingling in his body.

He caught Hadad just as the man reached the alley, shoving him to the ground again. He jumped on top of Hadad just in time to land on Hadad's upraised knee. The blow hit Jake in the liver, and his body shivered as pain worse than anything he'd felt since St. Clair stabbed him rushed through his body. He staggered and only barely dodged the blow Hadad threw at his head. He didn't dodge the foot Hadad stuck out though, tripping and staggering backward, giving Hadad time to get to his feet.

As the fight wore on, Jake kept waiting for instinct to take over.

There was always a point in hand-to-hand combat when he could stop thinking and just act. In most cases, hand-to-hand combat really meant knife combat. Short, brutal and effective. Jake had been trained more extensively in unarmed combat than most Marines, but it was never a priority. Almost no jarheads progressed past basic unarmed combat abilities. Absent specialized combat requirements, there was no need. That meant what they learned was simple, basic, and boring. If a Marine fought empty-handed, he was doing it wrong.

Jake had done a great deal more than that because of his regular forays into special forces work outside of the marines and his training with the Secret Service had further enhanced his skill set, but even in the Secret Service, Jake's training almost always involved a weapon of some sort.

Jake tried to reach for his combat knife, but doing so left his left side open. Hadad landed another blow to Jake's vulnerable midsection, and Jake cried out and collapsed to the ground. He was able to draw his knife, but Hadad quickly stomped on his hand and forced him to release the blade. He kicked it away and lifted his boot to stomp on Jake.

Jake burst upwards, driving one fist in between Hadad's legs. The man's eyes popped open, and he released a thin wail like a tea kettle just about to boil. Jake landed two quick blows, one to Hadad's liver and another to his jaw. The man dropped to the ground, but when Jake jumped on top of him and reached for the detonator, Hadad grabbed Jake's wrist and switched his hips, rolling him onto his back with Hadad on top.

The weight on Jake's midsection was staggeringly painful. More importantly, it didn't feel to him like he could get his head wrapped around the situation enough to take definitive action. The instinct he hoped for wasn't coming to him. He realized grimly that despite his extensive combat experience, he wasn't used to fighting hurt. He couldn't find the rhythm he typically could because his body wasn't used to operating under this kind of pain.

How fucking ironic would it be if I died here? The only Marine on Earth to be beaten by pain.

There was an old proverb used by Marine Corps drill instructors that said, "Pain is weakness leaving the body." Jake sincerely hoped that was true because if it was, he'd leave this engagement looking like a powerlifter.

He could hear civilians. There was laughter and conversation. There was joy. There was some grief and anger sprinkled throughout too from mourners who came to weep over the devastation of the last attack.

But there was no fear. The civilians remained completely oblivious to the fight happening in close proximity. They remained completely unaware of the stakes of the battle as well.

Jess's voice came over his earpiece. "Jake, don't overthink this. This is what you were trained to do. Just pretend this man is trying to assassinate the President. Actually, you don't have to pretend. He's tried three times already. Protect the President."

Jess's exhortation broke through the pain-induced fog in Jake's brain. Instinct took over finally. He bucked his knee up, trapped Hadad's elbow and ankle and rolled over. When he was on top of Hadad, he drove his fist into the man's face once, twice, three times.

With the third blow, Hadad's eyes rolled back in his head. Jake steadied himself and reached for the detonator again, but Hadad came to before Jake could take it from him. With a cry, he kicked Jake off of him.

Jake rolled to his feet, but the impact with the ground caused his teeth to chatter. The pins and needles in his body were more like spikes and drillbits now. He must have suffered nerve damage, either a lingering effect of the virus or caused by his several combat actions since Hadad's first attack on the President.

Hadad reached his feet the same time Jake did. He threw a haymaker, and Jake ducked to avoid it before launching himself forward at an angle. His shoulder impacted Hadad's solar plexus. Hadad's breath rushed from his body. That felt satisfying. *Now you know how it feels.*

Hadad staggered backwards, gasping for breath, but Jake didn't come away from the confrontation unscathed. A wave of nausea coursed through him, and any advantage Jake might have gained from ramming against Hadad.

He backed away, swinging wildly. That was pathetic, even for someone with limited hand-to-hand experience, but if he could at least keep Hadad away while he recovered, it would be worth it.

He felt pleasantly surprised that his fist struck Hadad's jaw. Unfortunately, it was only a glancing blow, and there wasn't much strength behind it. It irritated Hadad more than anything else. Hadad lashed out and landed a glancing blow against the side of Jake's head. Both men slowed. Hadad took a step back to collect himself, and Jake stepped back in the opposite direction.

What the hell? Is Bard offering combat classes to Trident friends and family?

The unpleasant thought occurred to him that Drew actually could train people in combat. Where was Drew? He had been around during the attacks in Washington, D.C. and Paris, but he hadn't shown any sign of himself so far.

He didn't get to speculate long on that though. A left hook from Hadad spun him around, and he had to focus on not going unconscious and firing back a right uppercut of his own. The uppercut hit Hadad, and the terrorist staggered backward, but either the pain in Jake's midsection had stolen his punching power or Hadad had a legendary chin.

Where's George Foreman when you need him? Jake thought.

It didn't make a lot of sense to him that the fight felt like one of those boxing movies. The end of the main event fight always worked the same way. The main character was tired. The opponent was tired. Some other character made a comment about the fight. It was down to who wanted it more. In those movies, it always came down to that.

Jake definitely felt tired. It seemed to him the only thing keeping him on his feet was determination. Maybe he really did just need to want it more.

Hadad appeared to be in similar or even worse shape. Jake mustered his strength and launched himself forward again. He jabbed twice toward Hadad's face. The man dodged wildly. It gave Jake an opening to land a very hard blow to Hadad's abdomen. He grunted as the air left him again. Jake felt another rush of satisfaction seeing Hadad's hands move to cover his injured stomach.

He followed up with a second blow to Hadad's jaw. He wasn't fighting on instinct anymore, but he was winning. That's all that mattered.

Hadad managed to land a wild blow to Jake's face. It staggered him, but it didn't matter. The battle was over or would be soon. Hadad had used up all the energy he had. Jake would likely have to spend some time recuperating after this fight, but he had enough energy to finish it.

He moved forward. Hadad performed a weakly executed kick at his legs. Jake easily stepped out of the way and landed two jabs to the terrorist's face. He landed a third as Hadad backed up, a stunned look on his face.

Then, as though just remembering he still had it, he reached for the detonator.

Jake lunged forward.

Tried to lunge forward. A wave of dizziness hit him. His vision grew blurry, and as he staggered backwards, his eyes fell. His shirt was soaked in blood. He realized dimly that he'd torn open the still-fresh scar from the knife wound he'd suffered in Paris.

He cursed, squeezed his eyes shut, and opened them again. He knew he'd pay for pushing through this, but the detonator took away any other choice.

Jess had said when, not if, he came back. For the second time in his life, Jake was sure he would have to break that promise.

Hadad flipped one switch. He reached for the other, and with a primal yell, Jake yanked the detonator from Hadad's hand, threw it on the ground and stomped on it.

If he had taken the time to think of that action, he wouldn't have done it. Many detonators had a failsafe that would trigger the bomb if the detonator was damaged.

Hadad's didn't. He stared in utter disbelief at the broken pile of wire and plastic. Then he looked up at Jake. "You asshole!"

Jake laughed. Maybe it was blood loss. Maybe it was pain. Maybe it was just the utter absurdity of Hadad's claim. "Oh yeah," he said, "*I'm* the asshole."

Hadad stepped forward. Then, for some reason Jake couldn't figure out, his eyes widened. Instead of finishing Jake off, he turned and ran.

Jake took a step forward and immediately fell to his knees. He felt strong arms around him and opened his mouth to say something.

But darkness took him first.

CHAPTER TWENTY ONE

Hospitals were the same everywhere. Jake didn't imagine that his thinking was particularly clever. For that matter, he didn't think his thinking was particularly clear. The blood loss affected him, and whatever medicine they had given him probably rivaled the painkillers that had Jess flying high at that very moment.

Or maybe not at that very moment. He had no idea how long he'd been here. The sense that his life hung in the balance seemed strong. He experienced too much clarity, though. If he knew his thinking was muddled, it wasn't really muddled, right?

"You just concentrate on getting well, Jake," Sheila said. He turned his head and saw her. He smiled as a rush of joy too powerful for any pain to drive away filled him. "Sheila," he whispered.

She smiled, and the love in her eyes made his painkillers utterly unnecessary. "Yes, baby. I'm here."

There wasn't worry on her face. There was sympathy. That meant his life didn't hang in the balance.

Wait a minute. He'd just arrived at the hospital. She wasn't allowed in the ambulance, was she? When has she arrived? Why was she here? How long had he been here?

He tried to sit up, but she put a hand on his shoulder. "Wait," she said, "let me help you."

She took hold of a remote attached to a thick, coiled cord. A moment later, he felt the top half of the bed angle upward. It lifted his torso to a reclining but no longer prone position. She handed him the remote. "Green arrow up does this," she said. "Yellow arrow down puts it back. The blue button turns on the television. The circle is channels. The triangle is volume. The little speaker button calls the nurse.

"How long?"

"About four hours."

He didn't speak. He'd slipped in and of consciousness. He thought he'd only been in the hospital for fifteen or twenty minutes. That was better than the two weeks he'd gone out in Paris, at least."

"And what about…"

"Hush," she said. Just in case he didn't intend to obey, she leaned forward and pressed her lips to his. "You just hush. Jess is working on things in Washington, D.C. Let her work."

"What about Jerusalem? Is everyone—"

"Everyone's safe. They found the bomb. It's some sort of advanced plastic explosive, but it's got nothing inside of it that can cause it to detonate anymore. It's completely inert. You stopped him."

He hadn't stopped Hadad. It was good to hear that he had temporarily foiled him, but as long as the man was at large, he hadn't stopped him. "Did they catch him?"

"Not yet." Her voice took on a touch of sternness. "No more work, Jake. You need to rest."

"But…"

She kissed him again to cut him off. There was a great deal of passion in her kiss, and he wished desperately that he were in any condition to do something about that passion.

She pulled her mouth away. "Hush. Jess can handle what needs to be handled right now."

"Okay," he said glumly.

Sheila smiled. "And now that you're awake, she's allowed to call you in an hour or so. I promised her I'd let her know. So, you won't be left out of the loop, but you're not getting up, and you're not leaving the hospital. You have to let somebody else save the world for a while, okay?"

"All right."

He said the words, but he knew there was nothing that would keep him from getting back into the fray if he had to. He knew Sheila knew that as well. She didn't call him out on it, though. Maybe she thought she could outsmart him and keep him here.

She said, "I'll call Jess, and then I promised to go call Dad. As for you, you don't have to be the one who saves the world. Not every time. Sit this one out for a while. You've done your part. Trust that other people are as capable of doing their jobs as you are of doing yours."

He didn't respond. He didn't want to make another promise they both knew he wouldn't keep.

"There are Mossad agents outside of this room with strict instructions to keep you here if you try to leave," she said.

So he was right. She thought she had outsmarted him. Hell, maybe she had. If he couldn't handle a two-bit arms dealer in a fight, he had less than zero chance against two trained Mossad agents. Hell, even if he was in top form, he probably didn't stand a chance. Mossad was one of the few agencies on Earth that actually did prioritize hand to hand unarmed combat in their training.

She leaned forward and kissed him softly again. She stood and surprised him, reaching into her pocket and pulling out his phone. She set it on the tray that held a pitcher of water and a plastic cup. "In case you decide to shock the world by not listening to me, you can involve yourself over the phone. But you *don't* leave this bed." She pushed the tray a little forward. "Green arrow up. Yellow arrow down." Then, after one last kiss, she left.

He stared in wonder after her. He looked at the remote device, but he didn't turn the television on. He considered it so he could potentially glean information from the local news, but before he could, his phone rang. Jess. He answered and she said, "You sound horrible."

"Thanks."

It's been an hour and a half. I wanted you to rest."

"An hour and a half?"

"Since Sheila called me."

He smiled. Sheila had called Jess even before he woke up. She knew he would want to dive right into the problem the moment he was awake.

Dammit, he loved that girl.

"What do you have for me?"

"Art is busy with damage control," she said. "The fact that Dalton made it into headquarters and all the way to my office unopposed revealed at best very poor security and at worst, the possibility that there are more insiders helping him."

That, unfortunately, made sense. "So he's combing through the ranks to find a traitor."

"Or traitors. I put a trace on everyone's phones and emails—personal and Service—and I have my friend at the NSA working on everyone's communications for the past year."

"Good job," he said softly.

"That's it. You need to rest."

"No. I'm good. Are you good? You were hurt too."

"I can hear that you're not good," Jess said, ignoring his query. "A five-year-old could hear that you're not good."

"Right now," Jake said, "Hadad is regrouping. Hell, he might be meeting with Bard. They might be busy framing this as a minor setback so they can get right back to work."

“And you’re not any good to anyone right now, Jake.”

“Are you?”

“We’re talking about you, not me.”

That was as clear an answer as any. “If you’re working through your injury, I can work through mine. We need to put a stop to Hadad and Bard. Clearly, you understand that we can’t rest. Please accept that I understand the same thing.”

Jess sighed. “Jake, you have nearly killed yourself several times. Don’t ask me how, but I got your medical record from the doctors in Jerusalem.”

“Jess—”

“Severe muscular damage, potentially permanent nerve damage, compromised digestion, damage to the pericardium—that’s the muscle surrounding the heart.”

“I know what the pericardium is.”

“Then you know you’re on death’s fucking door!” Jess shouted. She sighed. “Jake, we need you alive. We’re not being sympathetic, and we’re not being selfish so we can keep a friend in our lives. We’re preserving an asset that has proven crucial in our fight against Trident. What would you tell an injured Marine who wants to lead a solo assault against an entrenched enemy position?”

Dammit. She had him there. He sighed and said, “I would tell him that it would be a waste of resource for him to recklessly get himself killed.”

“And you’d be right. So, Senior Special Agent Mercer, don’t waste our resources.”

He didn’t have a good comeback to that. “All right.”

“I think you mean yes, ma’am.”

He smiled. “Yes, ma’am.”

“Better. Now, do you want to know what we’ve learned or not?”

“I mean, probably not, but I guess I have to.”

She giggled, and Jake’s smile widened. He wasn’t sure how he could feel so good right now with everything going on. It must be the drugs.

“I’ll start with the bad news, then I’ll give you the really bad news.”

“Goody.”

"I know, right? So, the bad news is that Hadad is far more entrenched than we initially believed him to be. Art's been handling most of that side of the investigation, and I have to say, he's a hell of a detective. I wouldn't have believed it, but he's not just a snobbish, self-important douchebag."

"I'll make sure to tell him that when I see him next."

"Go ahead. I already told him. Anyway, he's learned that Hadad has connections throughout the government: Congress, the military, the Secret Service—we knew about that—and possibly even the CIA."

Jake frowned at that last part. The CIA was notoriously hard to infiltrate successfully. Not that CIA operatives were unusually loyal, but the nature of the agency's job was such that it was almost impossible to act traitorously without raising considerable red flags. If Hadad really did have contacts in the CIA, then he was well-entrenched indeed.

That raised another question. "Is it possible that Bard is using Hadad for his network and not for his arms or his personnel?"

"I think it's a combination of both. The more I play the events of the past two weeks in my head, the more I think that Bard and Hadad have a better working relationship than Bard hinted at."

"So why did Bard give us accurate information about the first Jerusalem attack?"

"That still stumps me. My best guess is that he thought that Hadad would succeed anyway. I figured he was doing what you said and trying to upstage us and show off."

That was possible. "So what's the really bad news."

"It's really bad, Jake."

"So, do you think I can know about it? I just saw Sheila, and she's on her way to see her father, so I can't imagine it's worse than I can handle."

"It's still bad."

"I still want to hear it."

"First, promise me that you'll stay where you are and preserve our valuable resource."

Jake sighed. "I promise I'll preserve our valuable resource."

"And?"

"That's the best I can do."

There was silence for a moment. Then Jess said, "All right. Hadad is planning an assassination attempt on the President in Washington, D.C."

Jake sighed. It said a few things—none of them good—that he no longer reacted in shock to such news. "How much do we know?"

“That’s it so far. We’ve gotten a schedule of the President’s planned public appearances from the White House Chief of Staff. We can’t tell at which of these events the attack will take place, though.”

“It might not be at an event.”

“True, but as you’ve said before, the President is most vulnerable. I have some thoughts. I’ll send them to you, but you need to rest first.”

“I don’t need rest,” Jake said.

But his eyelids grew heavy, and ten minutes after Jake hung up, he was out like a light.

CHAPTER TWENTY TWO

It felt a bit strange to wake in a gentle way. The dawn light filtered through the window. Jake felt almost comfortable as his eyes opened. He hated to accept that he needed this time. On the other hand, his stubbornness no longer extended to stupidity. Over most of this trip, he'd questioned how long he would be able to keep up the pace. He'd expected exhaustion to take him, mental if not physical.

He had no choice but to accept that he needed the rest. This was the first time he could point to in recent memory where rest seemed more important than anything else. Enjoying rest brought its own kind of trepidation, but he didn't mind. In fact, he felt good.

Part of the reason he felt good was the progress that Jess and art had made. Art had already identified two Secret Service agents and a congressional staffer who were working with Hadad. After a show of bravado, Art had kindly reminded them that if they didn't share what they knew, they would spend the rest of their considerably shortened lives as test subjects for the CIA's interrogation tactics. He then asked if they felt they could escape the way Bard had. They did not feel that way and chose instead to reveal a great deal of useful information about Hadad's resources.

Hadad still had considerable influence, but he had lost a lot of manpower thanks to Jake's actions in the Middle East. He could act, but he could no longer act on a grand scale.

His phone rang, interrupting his thoughts. That was jarring when compared to the soft way he woke. The sound was grating. He sighed and grabbed it. Jess. All of the calm was gone now, and he realized with some irritation that he felt good, not because he was still kept abreast of the situation but because he could feel removed from it for a moment. The image of he and Sheila in their cabin in the woods floated enticingly across his mind. Maybe someday.

"What've you got?" he asked.

"We have new details on the plot."

"Okay."

"Assassination, I mean."

"Yes," he said. It took a great deal of effort not to make a smart comment about that. What the hell else were they talking about?

Maybe it was just because he was on weaker painkillers now that he was so irritable. "Tell me about it."

"You have to help remotely."

"What are you talking about?"

"That was the deal I made with Davis that let me call you. You can help, but you do it remotely."

"I don't help. I run the operation," he said. "I coordinate and I command, Jess. I'm not helping."

"Yes," she said. "I'd forgotten that your middle name was Jehovah. The important thing is that you can't leave the hospital bed, okay?"

That was irritating, but it made sense. "Okay. Tell me now."

"He's planning to assassinate the President at the State of the Union address."

Jake sighed. "All right. Have Dawson transport the President to Outpost Alpha and surround it with the most capable agents we have. Call the Pentagon and ask them if they have any bored Delta Force agents who want to play hunt the terrorist."

There was a pause that was just long enough to tell Jake that Jess was about to give him more bad news. "He's giving the speech outside at the National Mall."

"Of course he is," Jake said with a cheerfulness that belied his anger. "After all, Bryan's fucking invincible, right? Tell Hadad to aim for the head. No bullet on Earth can enter that thick of a skull."

Jess didn't reply. After a moment, Jake sighed. The sheer number of assassination attempts was getting to him. If this went on long enough, one of them was certain to succeed, right? Damn it, this was getting to be too much.

Getting to be? Hell, it was already too much.

He fought back those feelings and asked as many questions as he could come up with in order to solidify his understanding.

"When's the speech?"

"Two days. Veterans Day."

"Christ, is it Veterans Day already?"

"No, Veterans Day is two days from now. Pay attention."

"Jess, I'm not in the mood."

"Hey, you deal with stress by being a grumpy asshole. I deal with stress by teasing you and making jokes. Get used to it."

He sighed. “Fair enough. Has Art come up with a security plan yet?”

“Not yet. He knows you’ll want control over that, so he’s waiting for your call. I called you first because I can deal with grumpy asshole Jake better than grumpier asshole Art can.”

“I mean this with much affection, Jess. Fuck you.”

“I mean this with much affection, Jake. Not even in your dreams, and I’m telling Sheila you asked.”

Despite his anxiety and irritation, Jake couldn't resist chuckling. "Well, thanks for the update, and thanks for putting up with my grumpiness. I promise it'll be worth it one day."

“I bet you tell all the girls that. I mean it, Jake. I hear you’ve left the hospital, and I’ll strip your Harley for parts and sell it at a loss to people you hate.”

“You’re evil.”

“And you’re stupid. Which sometimes necessitates evil behavior from me.”

Jake chuckled again. “Well, thank you anyway. I’ll call you again after I’ve talked to Art.”

“Sounds good.”

Jake called Art, and when the director answered, Jake said, “First things first: I’m running this from our command center in Jerusalem.”

“We still have one?”

“We will after I talk to Mossad and get one. I can’t run an op from the hospital. I need computer screens and real-time information.”

“You have Jess for that.”

“Art, this is happening. You can fire me for it later, but I’m well enough to stand and walk, and that means I’m well enough to run the show from the situation room, not a hospital room. I won’t fight anyone, I promise. I’m six thousand miles away from anyone to fight as it is. If you insist, I’ll go right back to the hospital after the President is safe, but I can’t lead—”

“Okay, okay. I get it. You need to wave your dick. Fine by me. Looks mighty big. Good for you.”

“Fuck you, Art.”

“You probably could considering how massive your schlong is.”

Jake chuckled. “I see Jess has been giving you help with your humor.”

“Turns out it’s a great way to deal with grumpy assholes.”

“Funny. She said the same thing to me.”

"That explains why she still has all her hair."

"That one might need a little more work."

"Screw you, Mercer. Look, at least take some painkillers before you leave. I'm not saying you need to turn yourself into a vegetable, but pain will impact your ability to make good decisions."

"I got it. I don't need you to babysit me."

"Then act like it."

Jake let the argument drop. "So I want a smaller scale version of what we had when Trident attacked the White House."

"Smaller scale?"

"But more mobile and streamlined. Fewer moving parts and fewer communication backlogs and crossed wires. We need all the same elements: air support, ground support, bodyguards, security, RRTs, you name it, but instead of a bunch of little chiefs, we have one chief. That's me. People do what I tell them to do, and there's no need for middlemen. We can react in real-time to threats instead of playing pass the baton."

"I like it in theory. Are you sure it will work in practice?"

"What would work is locking the President onto a chair and wheeling him in front of the cameras in Outpost Alpha every time he needs to communicate with the public. Unfortunately, I'm told that's called staging a coup, and is, in fact, treason."

"I see Jess has been helping you with your humor."

"Nope. That's all me. Just because I don't use humor doesn't mean I don't have it."

"So you choose to be an asshole. Good to know."

"What's your excuse?"

"One day, Jake, you will be a deputy director like me, and when you are, you'll know the answer to that question. I'll call you later when I have details."

"Thank you, Art."

When Art hung up, Jake sighed and lay back in his bed. He had accomplished a great deal, but it had taken a toll. His breathing was labored, and the dull throb in his abdomen told him in no uncertain terms that he needed to stop being an idiot and give himself a real chance to heal.

But he couldn't. He couldn't allow anyone else to run this show. He had faith in his colleagues' abilities, but they couldn't replace him.

He called Jess when he was finished with Art, as promised. "How is tracking coming along?"

She had something going on, a routine or maybe a subroutine. Hell, he didn't know. She had her computer at headquarters doing something, though, to track communications and, hopefully, to come up with a location for Hadad. If she could come up with that location, they might be able to behead the snake before it struck. He had no idea if that analogy worked, but it sounded good.

"Let me dial in," Jess replied. He felt a wave of pain course through his spine and gritted his teeth against it. He didn't want her to hear in his voice the pain he felt.

"I've got him," Jess said. "I've got GPS coordinates for the last several communications."

"Send out a death squad," Jake said.

She laughed and said, "Don't I wish. Any agents in particular?"

"You know who's dedicated as well as I do. I want reliable people on this, though. I don't want him to slip through the cracks. Not an RRT, though. They're more like hammers. We need a screwdriver right now."

"*I* need a screwdriver. And a whiskey sour. And a gin and tonic. And an entire bottle of tequila.

He took a breath and then said, "And wait. Don't brief anyone until right before the mission."

"What? Why?"

"I don't want to risk Hadad catching wind of it before we go after him. He has too many people on his payroll. We can't be sure we've gotten all of them."

"Right. You got it."

She hung up, and while she was away, Jake made arrangements for transportation.

Not to the command center in Jerusalem, though. He knew he would catch hell from everyone when he showed up to headquarters in Washington, D.C. tomorrow, but he couldn't stay away. The more he thought about it, the more he thought Bard really was trying to separate him from his companions. He had done that now, and as much as he trusted his team, he knew he was the best chance they had at stopping Bard.

He dialed a familiar number. A moment later, Max Harrison—Jake's best friend and former mentor in the Marine Corps—answered the phone.

"Max, I need to call in a favor."

"As in a *favor?"*

"Yes."

"Damn. Okay, what is it?"

"I need a flight home."

Max didn't answer at first. When he did, his voice was deadly serious and more than a little irritated. "You know I could get in a lot of trouble if I'm caught helping you do this, right? You're under strict orders to remain in Jerusalem."

"Yes. That's why I'm cashing in a favor. You owe me three the last time I checked. I'm cashing in one of them."

Max sighed. "If you were anyone else, I'd tell you to go to hell. But I do owe you. All right. I'll make some calls."

"Thank you."

"Don't thank me yet. I'm pretty convinced I'm about to get you killed. Just so you know, if you *do* die, I will loudly proclaim 'I told you so' to everyone at your funeral."

Jake smiled. "You'll have to get in line."

"Yeah, yeah. I'm sure. Good luck, Jake."

"Thank you, Max."

Jess called just as Max hung up. "All right. I put a team together."

"Outstanding. I'll see you soon."

"Sounds good. Wait. You'll what?"

"I'm coming home, Jess. Don't try to stop me."

"Jake…"

"I can't just sit here and wait, Jess. The President is in danger. Hell, a lot of people are in danger. I have to be there."

"Jake…"

"You'd do the same thing if you were in my shoes. You can't ask me to sit in a comfortable bed when others are risking their lives."

"Jake!"

"What?"

"Just… take care of yourself. Okay?"

Jake felt a stab of guilt when he said, "Of course. I promise."

"Good. If you die, I will shout, 'I told you so' at your funeral."

Jake laughed.

"What's so funny? I mean it, Jake."

"I know. That's what's so funny."

"You're stupid."

"I love you too."

"Don't say that! God, is Sheila there? Can you put her on speaker?"

Jake's smile faded slightly. Sheila. She was still talking with her father. He would have to tell her he was leaving, and when he did, she wouldn't be happy.

"I'll see you later, Jess."

"You better. If you die, so help me… well, you know."

"I do. I really do."

CHAPTER TWENTY THREE

In general, all-nighters didn't work. Cramming for exams didn't work. Finishing a term paper on the last night… any of that. It sure as hell didn't make sense now. If Jake couldn't trust an all-nighter for something like a midterm, how could he trust it for this? The President's life was at stake. This wasn't a test. It was the principle of diminishing returns.

It was not for lack of effort or will. It had nothing to do with skill either. There were only so many sensory inputs that his brain could effectively process. As that diminished, his productivity would diminish. In the beginning, an hour of work was an hour of results. Hour eight might produce forty minutes worth of results. During an all-nighter, results crawled. There was a limit. Beyond that limit, a brain simply couldn't keep up.

Still, as he approached hour eleven of the all-nighter, Jake felt better than he had in days. He might not quite be a hundred percent, but he was far better than he was when he woke up in the hospital in Jerusalem two days ago. The ache in his abdomen was no more than an itch now, and the doctor had told him he was healing far faster and better than expected when he released Jake.

He could do this.

Besides, he didn't need to process new information. He needed to prepare a security plan. That took far less mental effort than analyzing data. If Jess could still do that effectively on the strength of three coffees, a donut and a ham sandwich, then he could put pieces where they belonged on a chessboard. He put a few finishing touches on his plan and finally slid a paper over to Jess. "Take a look."

"Your handwriting sucks, Jake," Jess said.

He wondered if the laughter in her voice had to do with relief that he was out of the woods or irritation that he was here in D.C. and not recuperating in the hospital as he had been advised. As far as his injuries were concerned, he was out of the woods anyway. The doctor had told him he was well enough to be released. Granted, he said Jake was well enough to be released to recuperate at home, but what Art didn't know wouldn't hurt him.

Art was pissed. He had berated Jake for a good ten minutes when Jake showed up out of nowhere, saying he decided to run the show from D.C. instead of Jerusalem, but Jake could tell by the way the director's shoulders relaxed that he was also relieved to have Jake here. Art was an excellent delegator. He was great at giving responsibility to the people best equipped to handle that responsibility. That was why he was a deputy director. Art had once been a great agent, but he didn't have the talent for managing a security scenario the way Jake did. So, although he was irritated at Jake for brazenly disobeying his instructions, he was relieved that Jake was here to do the job he was best at.

Sheila was another story. She had kissed Jake goodbye, but she was stiff with anger in his arms. Her last words to him when he left were, "One day, Jake, you'll realize how foolish you've been. I hope that day doesn't come too late."

That was a very dark cloud to an otherwise very bright silver lining, but he would deal with that later. Right now, he had a President to protect.

"You've got layers on top of layers," Jess said. "Redundancies on top of redundancies. What happened to a simple plan?"

"I want to keep this between as few people as possible. The simple plan is to fool the moles."

"How are people going to execute this plan, though? If they don't even know what's expected of them, how can you expect them to do their jobs properly?"

"Most of the complexity is stuff you and I are handling ourselves. I've kept the specific tasks of the agents assigned to this operation relatively simple. It's more work for us, but it provides a layer of protection against sabotage and double-crossing. The only risk right now is that Hadad might have paid one of our own to carry out the assassination. If he did, I have a countermeasure for that too."

"And does Art know that your friend, Max, will be acting as a sniper?"

Jake had called in one of his other favors. He was down to one, but since he still wasn't a hundred percent, he wanted a steady hand holding the rifle that would watch out for any sign of an assassin approaching the President.

"He does not, and if all goes well, he won't. If all doesn't go well, he'll be perfectly happy to know that the would-be assassin was killed. I'll get another lecture. That's it."

She stared at him a moment. Then she sighed. "You're incorrigible. Fortunately for you, I can get the surveillance set up. There's a lot of work, but it's not going to be hard, just a lot of it."

He marked various places on the paper with a highlighter. "We need agents here, here, here, here, and here," he said. "They need to have explicit instructions to watch a particular section of the crowd for potential threats."

"Got it."

"And we only deal with agents we trust," he said.

She nodded. "Yes, we went through that part. I vetted everyone thoroughly.

"Even if we trust them," he continued. "They get only their instructions. I don't want anyone to know what anyone else is doing."

"Understood."

She wore a slightly nauseous expression that he understood completely. It was sickening to not be able to trust their colleagues. A few months ago, he would have trusted any of them with his life. Now, he wasn't sure of anything. Perhaps only Jess and Art deserved that kind of trust without hesitation.

"Jess," he said, "one more thing."

"What's up?"

"As the day progresses, there is going to be more and more urgency. Nerves are going to be frayed. We can't help that. You and I, we need to keep cool. We need to focus on the task at hand and nothing else. As long as we're doing that, we can corral the rest of them and get them doing what they need to be doing."

"You're seriously going to talk to *me* about controlling my emotions? Get fucked, Jake. And not in the fun way."

"You don't know what I like."

She rolled her eyes, but he saw the smile playing on her lips before she could hide it. "I'll bet I know more than you think."

"What?"

"Nothing. Now screw off and let me work."

Jake headed to the break room for more coffee and a breakfast sandwich. He was tense, but he was no longer anxious. They'd done all they could.

Yet again. Jake felt a little bit like the guy from a movie reliving the same day over and over. The movie was a comedy. Jake felt like he was in a horror film.

"Well, if I am, then I'm the guy who keeps beating all the space aliens that jump out at you from eggs."

"That was a girl!" Jess called through the door.

Jake reddened when he realized he'd said that out loud.

The speech would take place in two hours. That gave them each time to nap before they had to get into position for the speech. Jake tried to sleep, but the nervous anticipation of the coming event prevented him from getting any rest.

He couldn't stay here. He couldn't stay still. Looking back on the past few weeks, what had frustrated him the most was the fact that he started most of these events somewhere far away from the action. He wanted to be down where it counted. He wanted to be able to respond to threats right away.

He sighed and left the sleeping Jess a note. Then he put on tactical gear and tested his mobility. His wound still hurt, but he could twist and turn and flex to a reasonable degree. As long as their killer wasn't some sort of parkour expert like St. Clair had been in Paris, he would be able to keep up with them.

He recalled his fight with Hadad in Jerusalem and reddened slightly even though no one was there to see him.

Well, that was different. He was in better condition now after nearly a week's rest than he was in Jerusalem when he fought Hadad. He would be all right.

More importantly, the President would be all right.

He gave one final look back at Jess before he stepped out of the room. She slept peacefully, and for a moment, it occurred to Jake that she was beautiful.

Then he left the room and a moment later, the building.

Jake reached the Mall fifteen minutes later. A crowd was already gathering, which surprised Jake. How easily people forgot. Only a few months ago, a terrorist attack barely a hundred yards from this very location had resulted in the deaths of six people, yet there were thousands more who believed that nothing bad would happen to them.

If only such delusions could be fulfilled.

To the credit of Jake's team, they immediately recognized him as a potential threat. Of course, they quickly identified him as one of their own, and when they realized exactly who he was, they reddened and stammered apologies that he quickly rejected.

"You guys are doing exactly what you're supposed to do. I don't care if the Vice President shows up; I want people talking to her before she gets within rifle range of the President."

"Where should we expect you, sir?"

"I'll be roaming," Jake said, "looking for potential threats."

His earpiece buzzed, "And when this is over, you'll be looking for pieces of yourself all over the Beltway. What the hell, Jake?"

"I couldn't sit still, Jess. I'm sorry. I had to get out here."

She sighed. "For fuck's sake. Fine. But if you die, I'll—"

"I know, I know. I told you so."

"Whatever."

"Jess, I'll be—"

"If you tell me you'll be fine, I'll make sure you aren't."

Jake was about to respond, but before he could, he heard the introductory speaker call the event to order. He mingled with the crowd, looking for any sign of someone suspicious. During the first two speeches, he saw only happy civilians enjoying a chance to see their great leader.

Jake knew better than to relax, though. All events like this went smoothly.

Until they didn't.

This one stopped going smoothly shortly after the President took the podium. Jake's earpiece buzzed, and Jess said simply, "White van. Eight o'clock, two hundred yards."

Jake turned and saw a man in a dark coat with a hat and sunglasses despite the cloudy day. From this distance, it was impossible to be sure, but he appeared to be holding a small box similar to the detonator Hadad carried in Jerusalem.

He looked around for assets, but he was the closest one to the van.

"Jake," Jess said, "Don't—"

But Jake was already on his way.

He reached the van just before the terrorist was able to press the detonator. The man looked up at Jake in shock, and through the disguise, Jake could see that it was indeed Hadad.

Hadad reached for the detonator, but Jake grabbed it first. He wrapped his left hand tightly around the box, covering the buttons, and pulled his handgun with his right hand, pressing it against Hadad's temple.

"Is it worth it?" he asked the terrorist. "Are you willing to die for this?"

Hadad looked at him, his expression seething with anger. He bared his teeth, and his finger twitched toward the grenade.

Then his snarl receded. The hate in his eyes slowly faded. He released the detonator, allowing Jake to take it. “It doesn’t matter,” he said. “You’ve ruined everything already.”

“Where’s the bomb, Hadad?”

“It’s in the Reflecting Pool. Enough C4 to blow up the entire Mall.”

“C4?”

Hadad smiled ruefully. “You’ve taken everything from me. I have no weapons anymore. Nothing of any consequence. I had a stockpile of plastic explosives, and I thought it might be worth Going out with a bang. But it doesn’t matter. I could kill everyone here, and it wouldn’t change anything. I’m done for.” Jake decided not to argue further. He turned Hadad around and handcuffed him, then radioed Jess. “I have Hadad in custody. The bomb is in the Reflecting Pool. Whole lot of C4. Evacuate the crowd and pull it out.”

“C4? Not that that’s not dangerous, but I kind of expected something a little more… is impressive the right word?”

Jake looked at Hadad. “No. That’s not the word I would use.”

EPILOGUE

Jake looked at Hadad and wondered how a man who was so dangerous could appear so normal. With all of the mystique stripped away, Hadad was nothing more than an average-looking man in his thirties with an inflated ego and a charismatic personality.

Now, he didn't even have that.

What really struck Jake was the difference between Hadad and Bard. Bard had acted defeated, but Jake hadn't believed it for one minute. Somehow, he knew that Bard would find a way to escape despite all of their best efforts.

And he had. Maybe it was a self-fulfilling prophecy, or maybe there was just a difference between someone truly dangerous and someone who was only playing at being dangerous.

Either way, the man who sat in front of Jake now was nothing like the man who was still out there concocting plans to assassinate the President at the cost of as many innocent lives as it took.

But maybe he could help Jake find that man.

"I'm not going to blow any smoke, Hadad," Jake told the terrorist. "You're in more trouble than you can deal your way out of. It's a toss up between life wherever the CIA feels like playing with you and a swift execution, and honestly, I'm not sure which is worse. What I *will* tell you is that if you hope to have any leverage at all over your fate, you need to tell me where Bard is."

Hadad scoffed. "And what do I get if I tell you what I know?"

"What do you want?"

"Your honesty. You promised me that much. Tell me what I could possibly hope for?"

Jake sighed. "You could possibly hope for life in ADX Florence."

Hadad laughed bitterly. "Oh, joy."

"Trust me. It could be worse."

"I'm sure it could. But the thing is, I don't know much that can help you."

"I'll take almost nothing if almost nothing is all you have. It's still better than nothing."

"Okay. Show me the paperwork that says I can get time at the supermax everyone knows about and not some secret death camp, and we'll talk."

"That's not how this works, Hadad."

"I know." Hadad shook his head. "I guess I just had to try. Old habits die hard. Well, I can tell you that you hurt Bard. Those men fighting for me? Those were his men, not mine. He's good at recruiting people, but even he can't sustain those kinds of losses. Trident was at one point the most numerous terrorist organization on Earth, unless you count a few groups in Africa, South America and the Middle East that are more properly described as guerilla armies. Now," he shrugged. "I'd be surprised if it's any more than Bard, Drew or Dalton."

"Did you have contact with Andrew McNeill?"

"Of course. He was Bard's lieutenant. I saw him more than Bard. Funny how leaders do that. They like to have middlemen relay their wishes to you. It makes them feel powerful. It's an oddly insecure trait."

"I find that most terrorists are insecure."

"But Bard isn't. That's his biggest strength, but also his biggest weakness. You know he couldn't believe that you beat him in Washington and France. He was amazed that you stopped the White House bomb. Utterly amazed."

"I remember. I saw him on TV."

Hadad chuckled. "Yes. He was quite upset about that. Made him look bad. Now that I think about it, maybe he is insecure. A narcissist, definitely. His ego bruises like a peach. May I have some water?"

Jake nodded at the stone-faced guard by the door. The man left the room and returned a moment later with a water bottle. He opened it and offered it to Hadad. Hadad somehow managed to drink without spilling water all over himself, no small feat considering his arms were shackled to the table by a chain that barely allowed him to rotate his wrists.

When he finished, he smiled and thanked the guard. The guard's expression didn't waver an inch from silent contempt.

"So," Hadad said. "The point is that he didn't believe he could be beaten. He believes so much in his cause that he has an almost religious certainty that things will work out in his favor. He doesn't know how to handle the fact that sometimes things don't work out in his favor."

"Drew," Jake reminded him. "Tell me about Drew."

Hadad looked shrewdly at him a moment. "He was your friend, wasn't he?" Jake didn't answer, and after a moment, Hadad said, "Well, he's not as interesting as Bard. He's just a bitter, hateful man trying to eliminate the source of that hate, or rather, what he thinks that source is."

"And what does he think the source is?"

"The government that betrayed him." Seeing Jake's expression, he said, "I know. It's gross. Childish, really. He's throwing a tantrum because Daddy spanked him for something he didn't do.

"Bard, however… he might be insane, but at least he has vision."

"What's his vision?"

"To create a fair and just government. One that rewards people for their contribution, not their connection, their capability, not their likability. A meritocracy of sorts. What he considers a meritocracy, anyway. It's all just drivel, of course. The world runs on greed. It always will until and unless humans evolve into a species whose origins don't lie in scarcity. There's a reason why ideal governments have never existed. People will always want more. But whatever. If Bard wants to believe he's the second coming of Jehovah, who am I to tell him he isn't? More money in my pockets."

"So that's what motivates you?" Jake asked. "Greed?"

"Of course. I'm human, aren't I?"

"Sure," Jake replied. "Whatever you need to tell yourself."

"Oh, my apologies, great saint, Special Agent."

Jake ignored the mockery and asked, "Where did you meet Bard and Drew?"

"They met me. I'm sorry, but if you're hoping to learn the location of their secret base, I don't have it. Between you and me, I don't think they have one. I hope they don't. They're caricatures enough as it is."

"What about future plans?" Jake asked. "Did they ever discuss that with you?"

"Ah," Hadad leaned back in his chair and grinned. "Now we're getting somewhere."

Jake fought to keep the excitement from his face. He kept his voice calm and said, "Could you expand?"

Hadad threw his head back and laughed. "My God, you're like a teenager on Christmas. You can't let on that you want desperately to know what that big box under the tree is, but you ask anyway, hoping that by appearing casual you might also appear mature enough to be entrusted with the secret."

“Close,” Jake said. “I’m more like the guy who gets to decide where you spend the rest of your life and how long that life is.”

“I doubt that. But I’ll indulge you. Bard, as I said, cannot conceive of failure. Drew, however, is more cunning. Having suffered great failure, he is more than aware of the fact that it is sometimes unavoidable. So, did Bard have plans for the future? No. But Drew? This is where his true value lies.”

“What were Drew’s plans for the future?”

Hadad steepled his fingers. “Bard thinks big!” He opened his hands as wide as his shackles would allow. “Drew thinks small.” He closed his fingers tightly and grinned. “Like a sniper! Like you! It’s funny, this struggle between you and Bard. It’s like the archer versus the dragon. The dragon is a massive and terrible beast. It weighs thousands of pounds and beats the air with its great rings. It bellows fire and breathes death. Its body is covered with armor so thick that it’s impenetrable by any weapon known to man.

“But one archer with one bow who’s brave and true, and just a little bit crafty and resilient can find the one small spot in that armor that’s weak, and with a single arrow, he can slay the dragon.”

Hadad leaned forward, his eyes glittering. “Bard is a dragon, Jake. But so is your President.”

He leaned back and said, “That’s all I can tell you. Send me wherever you wish. I made my peace with my fate a long time ago.”

Jake sat where he was for a moment. Then he pressed the intercom button and said, “Prisoner is ready for transport.”

Three more guards entered, and together with the fourth guard, they wheeled Hadad from the room. Jake remained where he was for a long time.

He wanted Drew for personal reasons, but he considered Bard the greatest threat. Could the real danger come not from the dragon but from the lowly archer who lurked in the dragon’s shadow?

NOW AVAILABLE!

ABSOLUTE PERIL
(A Jake Mercer Political Thriller—Book #4)

"Thriller writing at its best."
--Midwest Book Review (*Any Means Necessary*)

From the #1 bestselling and USA Today bestselling author Jack Mars (with over 10,000 five-star reviews) comes a groundbreaking new political thriller series: when the President of the United States or his family are threatened, it is up to Jake Mercer, former Marine sniper turned Secret Service agent, to protect them from dangers—both foreign and domestic.

As Air Force One soars towards Hawaii, Secret Service Agent Jake Mercer uncovers a plot to crash the plane. Can he protect the President and his family in this race against time?

"Thriller enthusiasts who relish the precise execution of an international thriller, but who seek the psychological depth and believability of a protagonist who simultaneously fields professional and personal life challenges, will find this a gripping story that's hard to put down."
--Midwest Book Review, Diane Donovan (regarding Any Means Necessary)

"One of the best thrillers I have read this year. The plot is intelligent and will keep you hooked from the beginning. The author did a superb job creating a set of characters who are fully developed and very much enjoyable. I can hardly wait for the sequel."
--Books and Movie Reviews, Roberto Mattos (re Any Means Necessary)

ABSOLUTE PERIL is the fourth book in a new series by #1 bestselling and critically acclaimed author Jack Mars, whose books have received over 10,000 five-star reviews and ratings. The series begins with ABSOLUTE THREAT (book #1).

A gripping and unpredictable political thriller, the Jake Mercer series is a page-turning action series that will leave you unable to put it down. This fresh and exciting action hero will have you turning pages late into the night, and fans of Brad Taylor, Vince Flynn, and Tom Clancy are sure to fall in love.

Future books in the series are also available!

Jack Mars

Jack Mars is the USA Today bestselling author of the LUKE STONE thriller series, which includes seven books. He is also the author of the new FORGING OF LUKE STONE prequel series, comprising six books; of the AGENT ZERO spy thriller series, comprising twelve books; of the TROY STARK thriller series, comprising seven books; of the SPY GAME thriller series, comprising nine books; and of the new JAKE MERCER thriller series, comprising five books (and counting).

Jack loves to hear from you, so please feel free to visit www.Jackmarsauthor.com to join the email list, receive a free book, receive free giveaways, connect on Facebook and Twitter, and stay in touch!

BOOKS BY JACK MARS

JAKE MERCER THRILLER SERIES
ABSOLUTE THREAT (Book #1)
ABSOLUTE DAMAGE (Book #2)
ABSOLUTE FORCE (Book #3)
ABSOLUTE PERIL (Book #4)
ABSOLUTE TREASON (Book #5)

THE SPY GAME
TARGET ONE (Book #1)
TARGET TWO (Book #2)
TARGET THREE (Book #3)
TARGET FOUR (Book #4)
TARGET FIVE (Book #5)
TARGET SIX (Book #6)
TARGET SEVEN (Book #7)
TARGET EIGHT (Book #8)

TROY STARK THRILLER SERIES
ROGUE FORCE (Book #1)
ROGUE COMMAND (Book #2)
ROGUE TARGET (Book #3)
ROGUE MISSION (Book #4)
ROGUE SHOT (Book #5)
ROGUE STRIKE (Book #6)
ROGUE ORDER (Book #7)

LUKE STONE THRILLER SERIES
ANY MEANS NECESSARY (Book #1)
OATH OF OFFICE (Book #2)
SITUATION ROOM (Book #3)
OPPOSE ANY FOE (Book #4)
PRESIDENT ELECT (Book #5)
OUR SACRED HONOR (Book #6)
HOUSE DIVIDED (Book #7)

FORGING OF LUKE STONE PREQUEL SERIES

PRIMARY TARGET (Book #1)
PRIMARY COMMAND (Book #2)
PRIMARY THREAT (Book #3)
PRIMARY GLORY (Book #4)
PRIMARY VALOR (Book #5)
PRIMARY DUTY (Book #6)

AN AGENT ZERO SPY THRILLER SERIES

AGENT ZERO (Book #1)
TARGET ZERO (Book #2)
HUNTING ZERO (Book #3)
TRAPPING ZERO (Book #4)
FILE ZERO (Book #5)
RECALL ZERO (Book #6)
ASSASSIN ZERO (Book #7)
DECOY ZERO (Book #8)
CHASING ZERO (Book #9)
VENGEANCE ZERO (Book #10)
ZERO ZERO (Book #11)
ABSOLUTE ZERO (Book #12)

Made in the USA
Coppell, TX
12 August 2024